TEMPTING DANGER

Katie Reus

Cover art: Jaycee of Sweet 'N Spicy Designs
Editor: Julia Ganis
Author website: http://www.katiereus.com

Tempting Danger/Katie Reus. -- 1st ed.
KR Press, LLC

ISBN-10: 1635560292
ISBN-13: 9781635560299

eISBN: 9781635560282

For all the readers who read Retribution and insisted that Andre and Alena get their happily ever after. This one is for you.

Praise for the novels of Katie Reus

"...a wild hot ride for readers. The story grabs you and doesn't let go."
—*New York Times* bestselling author, Cynthia Eden

"Has all the right ingredients: a hot couple, evil villains, and a killer action-filled plot. . . . [The] Moon Shifter series is what I call Grade-A entertainment!" —Joyfully Reviewed

"I could not put this book down. . . . Let me be clear that I am not saying that this was a good book *for* a paranormal genre; it was an excellent romance read, *period.*" —All About Romance

"Reus strikes just the right balance of steamy sexual tension and nail-biting action. . . .This romantic thriller reliably hits every note that fans of the genre will expect." —*Publishers Weekly*

"Prepare yourself for the start of a great new series! . . . I'm excited about reading more about this great group of characters."
—Fresh Fiction

"Wow! This powerful, passionate hero sizzles with sheer deliciousness. I loved every sexy twist of this fun & exhilarating tale. Katie Reus delivers!" —Carolyn Crane, RITA award winning author

"A sexy, well-crafted paranormal romance that succeeds with smart characters and creative world building."—Kirkus Reviews

"*Mating Instinct*'s romance is taut and passionate . . . Katie Reus's newest installment in her Moon Shifter series will leave readers breathless!"
—Stephanie Tyler, *New York Times* bestselling author

*A*lena *squeezed her sister Nika's thigh as she slid into the seat next to her. In the luxurious dining room of Andre Makarov—son of her mortal enemy—she could barely contain the nervous energy humming through her. The time was finally here. The man who had helped murder her parents was going to die tonight. After years of wanting revenge, it was finally happening. Her sister was nervous, and Alena couldn't blame her.*

Alena also hated that she'd dragged Nika into this. But there was no going back.

Out of the corner of her eye she saw her sister drinking her wine, her hand trembling slightly.

Next to Alena, Andre, the man she was dating—and using as a means to an end—took her hand in his. For a brief moment she savored his touch, squeezed his hand gently. She almost wished he was more like his father. It would make using him a lot easier. As it was, he was a good man. Which made this so much harder to do. But there was no going back now.

Sitting in Andre's formal dining room, surrounded by security—including Declan, the man her sister was now involved with—she was directly across from Yasha.

A monster.

It was inconceivable to her how Andre was so different from the other man, considering Yasha was his father. Andre

7

might be a ruthless businessman but he hadn't killed or tortured people to get where he was. No, he'd just worked hard.

Tall and blond, Yasha looked so much like his son, but his eyes were darker. And empty.

"How is your sister?" Yasha asked Andre abruptly, his voice slightly accented.

The change in Andre's posture was immediate. He went silent, his jaw tightening as he stared at his father. His knuckles clenched so tightly around his tumbler she thought it might crack. But he didn't squeeze her hand, clearly not wanting to hurt her. "She's fine."

"Please tell her I was asking about her well-being."

"Damn it, Father," Andre muttered.

Yasha suddenly swiveled to look at her, giving Alena all of his attention. It was jarring to be looking at him head-on like this. The man who'd raped her mother, killed her. Killed her father. Left her and Nika orphans. "He chooses his half-sister over his own father. She's nothing more than the daughter of a whore."

Alena stiffened. Under any other circumstances, she would have thrown her drink in his face and gotten up and left. But she needed to make sure he was dead. She'd sprayed poison on his fork. He would have a heart attack not long after his first bite. She couldn't risk Andre kicking him out, or anybody else coming in contact with that fork. Not when she'd finally come so close.

Andre slammed his fist against the table, making all of the silverware tremble under the force. "Damn it! Can't you just *behave like a normal human being for a couple hours? Why are you even here—"*

Though it was hard to do, she swallowed back her temper. "Andre." Alena placed a soothing hand on his forearm, hoping he would remain calm. He stilled immediately and she nodded toward one of the servers. A man dressed in all black was moving out of the kitchen, two salad plates in hand.

Oh God, this was it. Finally, her parents would have justice.

Next to her, Nika made a sort of strangled sound under her breath. Alena barely heard it though. All her focus was on the monster sitting across from her.

Soon you'll be dead. And I'm going to enjoy watching you gasp out your last breaths.

Yasha picked up his fork and looked between Andre and her, his expression calculating. "Maybe you're just a common whore too, Alena."

Andre stood, shoving his chair back. It clattered loudly against the beautiful custom hardwood floor. "That's it! Get the hell out of here right now."

Alena shook her head and held out a placating hand. "It's okay. He's just being protective of his son. Let's just eat and everyone will calm down." Ugh, were those words really coming out of her mouth? Patience, she reminded herself. Patience.

As Andre went to pick up his fallen chair, Yasha stabbed a piece of lettuce with his fork.

Adrenaline pumped through her, accelerating her heart rate. Eat it, you piece of shit. Eat it! *she silently screamed. His death would appear to be an accident. Once he was gone, maybe she could finally get on with her life. Maybe then she could find some peace. She'd already killed the other three men involved in the murder of her parents—and the rape of her mother.*

"Stop!" Declan shouted from beside Nika, his voice making the room go quiet.

Everyone turned to stare at him and Alena's heart stuttered when she saw his dark, angry expression.

"Drop your fork, Yasha." Declan's voice was razor sharp.

Oh no. *The security guy. The man her sister was sleeping with. He knew somehow. Oh my God, Nika had told him?*

"You told him?" Alena turned to stare at her sister in horror. Of anyone, she would have never expected Nika to betray her.

Nika shook her head, clearly trying to get her to be quiet. Oh hell. *Nika hadn't told, and now Alena had just given them away. He would never take the poison now.*

"Told him what?" Yasha asked as he laid the fork down, eyeing both of them warily now.

A surge of rage and pain like she'd never known welled inside her like a tsunami. No! She wasn't letting him get away. Not bothering to respond, she grabbed the nearest steak knife and lunged across the table at him like a woman possessed.

She was vaguely aware of glasses and plates scattering, of wine splashing all over her, but nothing mattered but plunging her knife right through his black heart. As she flew through the air, a hard arm snagged around her waist, jerking her to a halt.

Andre.

Struggling against his hold, she kicked out, sending one of her shoes flying and just missing Yasha's head. "Let me go!" she screamed as—

Alena's eyes snapped open at the sound of her phone's alarm going off. Heart racing, she sat up in bed, shoving the covers off her sweat-covered body. It had nothing to do with the late August New Orleans heat. She had the air conditioning cranked up so it was a cool seventy-two inside.

But after that nightmare—which was really just a memory—she always woke up agitated. Because it always ended the same. With Yasha walking out of that room alive and well. At least he'd died later that same night. He'd wanted to kill her right then but Andre had stopped him. If he hadn't, Alena had no doubt Yasha would have come after her eventually.

But Alena had still lost Andre, a man she'd initially only planned to use then walk away from.

Instead, she'd fallen in love with him. He didn't even want to see her, let alone speak to her. Not that she could blame him.

Except now she was three months pregnant with his child. And he had no clue. She wasn't even sure how to tell him. She was certain that he would hate her even more than he already did. Soon enough, however, she'd have to deal with him.

But it wouldn't be today.

CHAPTER ONE

One month later

Alena texted her sister as the driver of her hired car
pulled into the driveway of Nika and Declan's
house. Situated in a quiet neighborhood in Coconut
Grove, the two-story house was surrounded by trees and
lush foliage. She'd visited once before, a month and a half
ago, right after her sister's engagement. Everything
looked the same.

As she got out of the back seat, her sister flew out of
the front door and raced down the walkway toward her.
Nika had left her dark hair curly, falling around her
shoulders. It suited her. She and Nika had the same caramel-hued skin, a mark of their mixed heritage. With
those sharp cheekbones and vivid green eyes, her baby
sister was stunning. She was also smart and kind. Declan
was a lucky man.

"Your man better be treating you right," she murmured as Nika practically tackle-hugged her.

Snorting, Nika squeezed tight, then froze for a second
before pulling back. Her eyes widened slightly before
dipping to Alena's middle. *Ah, crap.* She'd worn a loose-
fitting, multicolored dolman-sleeve top that did a great
job of hiding her small baby bump. Clearly Nika wasn't

fooled. But her sister wouldn't say anything in front of a random driver. Not when anything about Alena could be leaked to the entertainment media. This guy probably had no clue who she was, but still, they'd always been careful about keeping their private lives private.

As Alena's driver shut the trunk and set her bags next to her, she swiped her credit card over his magstripe reader and included a nice tip. "Thank you."

"I can't believe you didn't tell me you were coming in early. Declan and I had already planned to pick you up," Nika said, lifting Alena's suitcase.

Since she was exhausted from the mere fact of being pregnant, she didn't try to take the big suitcase. Instead she picked up her much smaller travel bag and followed her sister up the walkway. Bright yellow roses grew rampant across the bushes lining the front of the house. They were her sister's favorite.

"I was able to get bumped up and didn't want to bother you guys," she said as Nika shut the front door behind them. "Your hair looks amazing," she added.

"Thank God for hair product for mixed chicks," Nika said, laughing. Snorting out an agreement, Alena started to respond just as Nika turned to her, eyebrows raised as she set the suitcase down on the wood floor of the foyer. "You're pregnant."

Yep. No hiding it anymore. "Four months."

Nika blinked once as she seemed to try to find her voice. "Oh my...oh hell...oh—"

"Nika. It's okay."

Her sister's eyes widened to cartoon proportions as something seemed to click. "It's Andre's!"

"Ah, yes. And no, he doesn't know. I'm definitely going to tell him. But he'll probably—definitely—want a paternity test, so I'm waiting for now." Because Lord knew she didn't need any extra stress in her life. Her doctor back home had been very clear on that point.

"But he's the only person you've slept with in...ages."

"I know that. And you know that. But he's not going to trust me." And she didn't blame the sexy billionaire. Not one bit. He might have no love lost for his dead father but Alena had tried to stab the now dead man...and she'd used Andre to get to Yasha. What a mess.

"Right. Well come on, I think you need to be sitting. I'll just grab these later." She waved a hand at Alena's suitcase and bag before linking her arm through Alena's.

"Or more likely, you'll just wait until Declan gets home and have him carry everything upstairs."

Nika laughed, the sound so open and refreshing. It warmed Alena straight to her soul. For so long they'd traipsed around the world taking revenge on the men who'd ripped their family from them. Their parents had been CIA agents, two of the best. One night four men had broken into their home and killed their mom and dad. Alena had managed to get herself and Nika hidden— even though she'd only been ten herself at the time—and when they'd finally emerged, it had been a bloody massacre. Alena had shielded her sister from seeing the carnage but those images had been seared into her own brain.

And she'd never gotten over it. Never been able to move past it. Not until recently.

"You know me too well."

As they stepped into the kitchen, a wave of nausea swept over Alena. Sometimes it happened like that. No trigger, no warning, just stupid sickness. "Bathroom?" It was all she could get out.

Nika must have read her expression because she pointed right back down the hallway. "First door on the left."

Alena actually knew that, had been in the house before, but she wasn't thinking straight right now. Less than two minutes later she'd emptied the meager contents of her stomach. All she'd been able to keep down was crackers anyway. After flushing the toilet then rinsing out her mouth with the little bottle of mouthwash on the counter, she splashed water on her face.

"Are you okay in there?"

Alena opened the door to find her sister standing there, her expression worried. "Yes. It's just morning sickness and totally normal. I just happen to get it in the afternoon, not the morning. By chance do you have any ginger ale or crackers? Or both?"

"Yep. Come on." A minute later Nika passed a can of ginger ale over to Alena where she sat at the center island. "So, you're really pregnant. That shirt does a decent job of hiding it, but with your slender frame, you won't be able to hide it much longer. In fact, I'm surprised it hasn't been posted on social media yet. Or by one of those gossip rags."

She took the drink gratefully, downing a quick sip before answering. As a model, every part of her was incessantly scrutinized. But lately she'd been lying low, and when her life was boring, no one paid attention. "It's because I've been hiding out at home the past month. About four weeks ago my belly popped and there was no way to hide it without loose clothing. So I canceled every future engagement—my agent knows why and is keeping quiet." She took another sip, glad it was helping settle her stomach. "I'll need to tell Andre before it hits the media. I'm just worried about his reaction."

Her sister's mouth pulled into a thin line as she nodded. Nika held a lot of guilt for the way they'd treated Andre. The man was so good and decent and Alena had stomped all over his heart. Yes, she'd done it so her parents would have justice, and yes, she'd been blinded by her need for revenge, but that didn't make her feel any better. She didn't feel guilty for what she'd done to the other three men involved and she also didn't care what that said about her. She could live with her actions. But she hated that she'd ruined that little bud of something real between her and Andre and that he now had a low opinion of her. God, what he must think.

"You might be surprised by his reaction," her sister said finally.

She gave a noncommittal shrug. "Maybe." She knew enough about Andre to realize that he wasn't going to be happy. But there was no way she was giving up this baby. She just hoped they could find a way to be civil to each other and make a co-parenting relationship work. If he didn't want that, then she was fine raising this child on her own. Since she'd stepped into her thirties, she'd been planning on slowing down in her career in the next five years anyway. Now was as good a time as ever. She had enough money saved and had made enough in residuals that she could afford to be a stay-at-home mom for a while. "I've been thinking of getting a place in Miami. I want to be closer to you anyway."

Nika's eyes widened in surprise as immediate pleasure flickered across her features. "I would love that. Don't get me wrong, I love Declan and his family is wonderful, but I miss you so much."

Her throat tightened with emotion at her sister's words. "I've missed you too," she said, wiping a few stray tears from her cheeks. "And FYI, I cry *all* the time now. It's like I'm a leaky faucet. I cried at a Doritos commercial the other day."

Nika rounded the corner of the island and pulled her into a hug. "Well those commercials can be sad," her sister said, only slightly laughing. "Now that you've opened the door for this move, you are definitely relocating here. I'm going to start looking at real estate!"

Laughing at her sister's enthusiasm, Alena just shook her head. She wanted to talk more about it, but more than anything, she wanted all the focus on Nika. "We'll discuss all that later. For now, let's talk about this wedding you're planning," she said as her sister pulled back. "You're going to make a stunning bride."

Nika rolled her eyes good-naturedly. "Honestly I'd be fine just doing a courthouse wedding, but Declan is very serious about having a church wedding and having all his brothers stand up with him."

"Good. It's what you deserve. I'm glad he's not letting you get off with a quickie wedding." She paused to nibble on a cracker. "How long is he willing to let you plan this thing? Two months?"

Her sister laughed. "Ah. One and a half. I swear that man is such a caveman. He says he wants to lock me down so everyone knows I'm off-limits. He's got the church and the reception venue reserved—apparently one of his clients owed him a favor so it's right on the ocean. And the guys already have their tuxes. You and I are the only ones who need to get dresses and he knows the owner of a bridal shop who will fit us in with no issues. It seems like a whole lot of planning for just one day."

Alena smiled. She was so glad her sister had found someone who treasured her for exactly who she was. "It's more than one day. If you guys couldn't afford it, then I'd say yes, skip all the fussy stuff but...he's your family now." Something she and Nika had never really had. "Doing something like this will be important to his side. You'll have no regrets." She wondered if Nika would take his last name, then immediately dismissed the thought. Of course Nika would. Soon she'd be Nika Gallagher instead of Nika Brennan.

"Yeah, you're right. And it's only going to be forty or so people so it won't be huge. I don't think I could handle that." Suddenly Nika's gaze turned sly. "Maybe I'll get to mark you down with a plus-one."

It took a moment for Alena to understand what she meant. "If you're talking about Andre, definitely don't get your hopes up." Even if Alena secretly hoped that maybe...one day he could forgive her, she was a realist.

Nika just made a *hmm* sound.

Deciding to ignore the Andre topic, Alena continued. "I swear, you really did land a good one with Declan."

"I know. Some days it's hard to believe. We've even helped the police with a couple cases. Off the books, of course."

Alena lifted an eyebrow but wasn't exactly surprised. Her sister was a psychic, as strange as that sounded to her. Years ago, Nika had been in a horrific car accident. She'd broken both her legs, ribs, and had suffered brain swelling. It had been one of the darkest times in Alena's life, thinking she might lose her baby sister. Ever since then, Nika had seen flashes of the future. Sometimes little premonitions, sometimes much bigger ones. They'd used her sister's gift when hunting the men who'd killed their parents, but she was glad that Nika was using it for something so positive. Declan had some psychic gifts of his own, too, so they were a perfect match. "That's incredible. I'm so proud of you. Will you invite Uncle Baxter to the wedding?"

"Of course. I miss him too. I've already given him a heads-up but I just need to let him know the actual date."

Alena had started to say more when she heard a little beep, indicating that the front door had opened. Less than a minute later, Declan stepped into the room. He smiled when he saw her and gave her a brief hug before moving right to his fiancée.

He might be wearing a suit, but there was an edge to him. A sort of roughness. He had an almost invisible scar next to his left eye and a slightly crooked bottom tooth that did nothing to take away from his looks. He was handsome, but not classically so and she was sure that he'd seen a lot of bad things when he'd been in the CIA. Not the kind of man Alena had pictured her sister ending up with, but he was perfect for Nika.

In the past, mostly when she and Nika had been younger, men had occasionally gone after Nika in an attempt to get to know Alena. Something that disgusted her to no end. Seeing Declan with her sister, there was no doubt that the man only had eyes for Nika. He was beyond smitten with her. "All right, you two, none of that in front of me. I—" She put a hand to her mouth as another wave of nausea swept through her.

"Really?" Declan's voice was dry as he raked a hand through his dark hair. "I can't actually make you sick."

Laughing lightly, she shook her head and pressed a hand to her stomach. "I'm pregnant."

His espresso-colored eyes widened. "What did Andre say?"

A ghost of a smile pulled at her lips. She was glad that Declan assumed it was Andre's, since it most definitely was. Despite her party girl reputation, almost all of it was fake. She'd cultivated her persona because it had been a lot easier to get into places when she'd been hunting the people who'd killed her parents. In reality she'd never done any drugs, and her lovers had been few. She'd always been incredibly picky. Though no one compared to Andre. "I haven't told him yet."

Declan simply nodded and expertly changed the subject. "Well, if you ladies would like, we can head out tonight for dinner or I'll order take-out. You're probably exhausted with all the travel so we'll leave it up to you."

Nika nodded along with him. "Yep, it's up to you, big sister."

"Take-out is fine with me, but I can only eat something really light. Maybe a Greek salad. Honestly I'd be fine with one of those salads from Publix. Also...tomorrow night I have a thing, a gala, I have to attend with a friend of mine." It was a risk going out with her small baby bump but she had the perfect dress to hide it. If the media bothered to speculate on her, they'd probably just think she'd gained weight. Which was apparently a mortal sin when you were a model.

"With who?" Nika asked.

"Nathaniel Johnson."

"Aww, I love him. He's one of the only decent guys you ever went out with. It's too bad there was never any chemistry."

"Agreed." Nathaniel was the sweetest man. And crazy wealthy to boot. But there had never been a spark between them. They acted as each other's plus-ones at events where they wanted to fend off unwanted advances. And Nathaniel had called in a favor. Considering he'd done the same for her numerous times, she hadn't been able to say no. And she missed him anyway. The past month she'd been holed up in her house, and getting out would be refreshing.

As Nika and Declan pulled out an array of take-out menus, talking about what sounded good, she contemplated calling Andre later that night. But no, this was the type of conversation that needed to be done in person. She just had to figure out a way to approach him, to say the actual words. From there... *Ugh.* Who knew what would happen.

* * *

Andre looked up as his assistant stepped into his Biloxi office. Instead of heading back to Vegas a week ago, like he should have, Andre had stayed at his other casino. Because it was marginally closer to a woman he *should* hate.

A woman he couldn't get out of his fucking mind. And he didn't hate her.

Barry hesitated in the doorway, something he never did. "I have an update on Ms. Brennan for you."

Fuck. Of course it had to be about Alena Brennan. Barry had never questioned why Andre wanted regular updates on the woman. Andre could tell himself it was because she'd lied to him, infiltrated his house and tried to kill his father—who was now thankfully dead, though not by her hand—but it was simply because he'd fallen for her.

Except he didn't know if he'd fallen for the real her or the lie. He'd replayed their time together over and over in his head too many times. She was beautiful, to be sure, but she was also smart. And she'd played very hard to get. He'd been up to the challenge of chasing her. When he'd finally caught her—he hadn't wanted to let go. Then everything had gone to hell. "What is it?"

"Her agent has canceled all her jobs for the foreseeable future. And she made a short announcement on social media that she was stepping back from work for the time being. No time frame given and no details."

That was interesting. Alena wasn't tall enough to be a supermodel but she'd made a big splash as a model for luxury items. Cigars, cars, a couple European clothing lines. It was no wonder. She was walking, talking sex appeal.

Everything about her was larger than life. She had high cheekbones, expressive dark eyes, naturally full lips, smooth caramel skin and an incredible body he knew that she worked damn hard for with Pilates and swimming. He resisted the urge to pull out his cell phone and look at the one photo of her he still had. They hadn't even been in a relationship long—not that it had been a real relationship. He thought it had been, but now he knew the truth. He'd been a means to an end for her, and nothing more.

Still, he hadn't been able to delete everything from their time together. Of course it was easy enough to go online and look up a picture of her, but all of those were airbrushed. He had something real. In the picture, she wore tight, dark jeans, knee-high boots and a belted coat with oversized sunglasses. Her lips had been painted a dark red, giving her a sultry look. He'd snapped it when they'd disembarked from his jet so many months ago. The first day they'd arrived in Miami together. He shook the thought off and focused on his assistant who was still talking.

"She's also…" Barry cleared his throat. "Ah, she'll be attending the conservancy gala, the nineteen-twenties-themed one, with Nathaniel Johnson in Miami tomorrow night. I heard it from a contact of mine."

Andre kept his expression neutral as he turned back to his computer. "Thank you. Call my pilot, tell him I'll be heading out later tonight. He needs to be on standby."

"Where will he need to file a flight plan?"

"Miami."

Barry simply nodded and stepped out of the office. Only once his assistant was gone did Andre shove back from his chair and stalk to the window that overlooked the biggest pool at the hotel. Shaped like a palm tree, with multiple cabanas surrounding it and a full staff, he was certain that everyone in the crystal clear, glistening water was enjoying themselves.

He wished he could enjoy himself too. But he'd been miserable for the last four months. He couldn't seem to get out of his own head. He was obsessed with thoughts of seeing Alena again.

And like a masochist, he was headed to Miami tonight in the hopes of seeing her tomorrow. *Pathetic.*

It didn't matter if it was, he was still going. He needed fucking closure. That was all it was. There were some things he wanted to say to her. Once he did, he'd be able to walk away. He was certain of it.

CHAPTER TWO

"What's going on with you?" Nathaniel asked as he and Alena stepped through a back entrance to the gala.

Arm slipped through his, she looked up at him. Even with her in heels he was much taller. It was a shame there wasn't any chemistry between the two of them. She knew for a fact she wasn't his type. He could have been hers. With an easy smile that hinted at a little wicked, gorgeous baby blues, and a lean, runner's physique, he could be any man or woman's type. Unfortunately, it appeared she only had one type. Andre.

"What do you mean?" she asked as they strode down a quiet hallway of the convention center.

The gala was in a huge ballroom closer to the front of the building, and she'd asked him if they could avoid the main entrance. She'd known there would be photographers there, mostly just local ones, covering this event for the local Miami outlets. But Miami was a glitzy, gorgeous place and occasionally paparazzi did show up, especially since more than a handful of actors and musical artists attended functions like this.

"Why didn't you want to walk in on the red carpet? For the record, I don't care, it just seems out of character."

She snorted softly at that. With her job, getting photographed publicly was often a good thing. Exposure and all that. "I just didn't feel like it. Thank you for understanding."

"You didn't have to come with me tonight." As they reached a set of double doors, he paused with his hand on one of them.

She could hear music and many voices just past the doors. "I wanted to. I've missed you."

He gave her an assessing look. "I've missed you too. And something is different about you."

During the time frame when she'd been hunting down her parents' killers, she hadn't seen much of Nathaniel. She'd sort of been avoiding him. She hadn't wanted to be around any of her true friends, the people she loved and adored, when she'd been on her quest for revenge. It had been easier to focus when it had just been her and Nika. "Good different?"

"I don't know. You look stunning as always. Does this have to do with you and Andre Makarov?"

She blinked at the question. He couldn't know she was pregnant…could he? Her dress was a deep blue with a beaded neckline and a tiered, fringed skirt that hid her baby bump well. The beaded design covered every tier so that the dress shimmered with every step she took. With a deep vee in the back and a low-cut neckline, she was almost guaranteed that no one would notice her bump. "Why would you ask that?"

He lifted a shoulder, apparently his only answer, and opened the door. As he did, he set his hand on the small of her back and ushered her inside. Immediately she experienced sensory overload. Rich, spicy scents of some kind of Cajun food filled the air, someone was playing a piano—the song simple, but something about it made her want to cry because lately everything did—and men and women dressed in fun nineteen twenties getup were everywhere.

"Two-step ragtime," Nathaniel murmured.

"What?"

"The music." He glanced down at her, that little smile playing at his mouth.

Damn it, life would be a hell of a lot easier if she was into him. "Oh...you didn't answer my question."

Lifting a shoulder, he scanned the crowd again as they moved through a throng of tables. He obviously knew where they were going. "When the two of you broke up, you never said much about it. That's not like you."

"Yeah." Her relationship with Andre had been speculated at in the media and on social media briefly but neither of them had made any public statements when they'd parted ways—ha, such a civilized way to put it— and everyone had quickly lost interest. He wasn't famous and she technically wasn't either. Yes, she represented exclusive, glamorous lines and she was often invited to parties all over the world, but she wasn't famous in the way actresses or supermodels were. She wasn't always recognized when she went out in public. She liked it that way. She made a nice living and could walk her dog without being harassed by paparazzi. If she had a dog.

"That's it? *Yeah?*"

Sighing, she looked up at her friend. Alena wasn't sure what he saw in her expression, but the flicker of pity in his gaze made her wince.

"Finally fell for someone, huh?" he murmured.

"Yep."

"He's a fool for letting you go," Nathaniel said.

"No, he's not." She glanced away from her friend, afraid she'd start crying if she thought too hard about Andre.

"Well, we'll agree to disagree. This is us." As they reached a table, he shook hands with a couple who she quickly learned owned their own law firm. The rest of the seats were empty but she was sure they would fill up soon.

Both men stood and shook her hand as introductions were made. As she sat, she moved the skirt of the gold tablecloth slightly so her heels wouldn't get caught in it. Everything was gold, black and glittery. A huge display of sparkly gold feathers erupted from a gold and black vase in the middle of the table.

The blond man, Steve, sat with her as his partner stood talking with Nathaniel. "Why do you look so familiar?" he asked.

She half-smiled. "Ah, I've done some modeling."

"That's it! I knew I recognized you. And you've done more than 'some.' I love that ad you did for...'"

She half listened as a wave of nausea swept through her. *No. No, no, no.* She would not get sick here. She simply couldn't. She'd already gotten "morning" sickness today. And she'd made sure to eat a little before she left so her stomach wasn't empty. But all these smells. The food alone was enough to make her react, but there was an array of perfumes filling the air. She didn't remember ever being so attuned to scents, but maybe her pregnancy had brought it on.

Whatever the reason, she didn't like it.

"How do you like living in Miami?" she asked, after answering a non-personal question about one of the designers she'd worked with.

"It's great here." He continued talking as the table started to fill up.

She was introduced to more people and was starting to feel a little better until she stood to greet a woman she'd met at another gala with Nathaniel a few years ago.

"Summer," Alena murmured, shaking her hand. "It's been a while. And you look fantastic." Tall, leggy, and lean, with jet-black hair falling in big spiral curls around her face, the woman definitely was that.

Summer narrowed her gaze slightly. "You do too, and I don't mean this as an insult but you look as if you could use some fresh air. It's the doctor in me."

At the woman's words, Nathaniel broke away from the man he was talking to. He shook hands with Summer as he looked down at Alena. "You do look a little pale.

Let's step outside for a minute. They have a patio area with music and food and it's right on the water."

Her instinct was to say she was fine but she nodded. And the thought of getting to breathe in the salty ocean air sounded like heaven. "I actually think that's a good idea." She'd taken one step with Nathaniel when one of her knees buckled. She had never fainted before in her life, and she wasn't sure if she was about to. But she knew she needed to get out of here right now.

Luckily Nathaniel caught her elbow and smoothly slid an arm around her so no one noticed anything—except the doctor.

"Change of plans," Summer said. "There are a couple private rooms here I've used before when guests needed to be checked out."

"Oh no, I don't want to take you away from the party." She clutched Nathaniel's arm, using him to steady herself. *And I don't want you examining me.*

"Well I'm not asking. I'm telling you," the woman said smoothly, her voice brisk but kind. "Let's do this."

Nathaniel was clearly concerned but smiled warmly at Summer. "Thank you. We'll just follow after you."

Alena had to force herself to take one step after the other as they moved through the throng of tables. They'd been there at least an hour and the crowd had definitely grown. Instead of the light ragtime music, a jazz band was performing, loud and boisterous. If she passed out or got sick here, someone with their stupid phone would take a picture. And it would somehow make its way online. She didn't want to risk that.

Just a few more minutes, she told herself. She simply needed to get out of the ballroom and somewhere private. If she threw up then, it would be embarrassing but it would be a lot better than hurling in the middle of a crowded dance floor.

As she and Nathaniel pushed through a particularly large crowd of people, she froze as they neared one of the exits.

Andre was standing by a full table, his hands shoved in the pockets of his slacks as he talked to an Asian man. As if he sensed her, Andre looked in her direction, pinning her with that icy blue stare.

Oh no, she definitely couldn't get sick now. Panic and nausea swirled inside her at the same time. What on earth was he doing here? She couldn't see him now. She wasn't prepared for this. *No, no, no.*

Andre's gaze swept over her and Nathaniel, no doubt taking in how close they were to each other. If anything, it probably appeared as if she was embracing him. Which she definitely was, but only because she couldn't stand on her own.

"We need to get out of here right now," she murmured. "I can't deal with talking to him or seeing him." Not here and not now anyway.

Nathaniel wrapped his arm around her shoulders and held her close as he continued steering them toward the nearest exit doors.

"It's just this way," Summer said, motioning down the hall and toward another set of double doors on the opposite side of the hallway.

Heart racing, Alena stepped inside with the other two. Summer grabbed a chair from a stack, and set it in front of her as Nathaniel flipped on a panel of lights. She instantly winced at the sudden onslaught as she adjusted to the brightness.

She already felt better being out of the loud atmosphere. Now she just needed to be alone for a bit. Sucking in a deep breath, she said, "I don't know if I can stay for the whole party, Nathaniel. I'm so sorry."

He waved her words away as he crouched in front of her. "I don't give a shit about that."

"How much alcohol have you had tonight?" Summer asked, pulling another chair up directly in front of her.

"Ah, none. And…I know why I'm feeling exhausted. And woozy." Sighing, she rubbed a hand over her clammy face. Right about now she wished she was back in her sister's guest room, wearing her pajamas, and sleeping. Or at least resting and bingeing on television. This pregnancy thing was no joke. And she was only at sixteen weeks. "I know you're not my doctor but—"

"Anything you say to me is confidential. And…" The woman's eyes flickered to Alena's middle for a fraction of a moment before returning to hold her gaze. "I think you just need to get some water and something simple to eat. But you definitely don't need to be here tonight if you're feeling exhausted."

"Maybe we should take her to see one of the doctors on staff, Summer," Nathaniel said. "I know you're good at what you do, but you're an OB. Maybe she should see—"

"I'm pregnant, Nathaniel." She hadn't planned to tell him like this, but she wasn't going to go see anyone else. She just wanted to leave. She would be asking for Summer's card though, since she was an OB. But the anxiety threading through her was starting to make her nauseous again. She needed to be gone right now. Far away from Andre.

"Pregnant?" Andre's familiar voice made her freeze before turning to look over her shoulder. Fear and a little mortification added to her anxiety. How was this happening?

Sure enough, he stood in the entryway, his expression darker than she'd ever seen it.

Oh, hell.

CHAPTER THREE

A ndre stared at Alena, sitting in that chair, her dark
eyes wide. "You're pregnant," he repeated. He felt
almost numb as he watched her. She was *pregnant.*

She glanced around, as if looking for an answer, but
he knew what he'd heard. When she met his gaze again,
she nodded and whispered, "Yes."

He knew without a doubt that it was his. He'd been
keeping tabs on her, knew that she hadn't been with anyone else. "Everyone else out," he ordered without looking at the others.

He knew the woman, Dr. Summer Freeman. Her reputation was solid. The man with her, Nathaniel Johnson,
was a successful businessman. He dealt in real estate and
architecture. He was also a pretty decent guy, and from
Andre's research, he knew that Nathaniel and Alena
were friends. He didn't think they'd ever been romanti-
cally involved but he also didn't like the possessive way
Johnson was hovering over her.

"You're the one who needs to get out," Johnson
snapped.

Alena laid a gentle hand on the man's arm as she
stood. When she did, Andre watched the way her dress
shifted slightly. Because of the tiers, it was difficult to see

any change in her body, though her breasts *did* look bigger. He frowned as Johnson turned toward her. "Get your hand off her." Technically Alena was touching Nathaniel and not the other way around, but seeing her with another man had him acting a little crazy. Not to mention the very important detail of her pregnancy.

Alena was having his child.

Looking almost exasperated, Alena dropped her hand and turned to the other man. "Nathaniel, Summer, it's okay. I need to talk to him."

Johnson looked at her, frowning. "I'll stay with you."

She shook her head before Andre could protest. "It's not necessary. Please wait in the hall if you would like. I really do need to talk to him. And Summer...I might call you next week."

"Please do. I'll probably get your number from Nathaniel and call you tomorrow just to check in. Are you sure you want to be alone with him?" she asked quietly but loud enough that Andre could hear.

He could respect that.

"I'm sure. He would never hurt me," Alena said quietly.

He internally recoiled at her words. Even when he'd been his angriest at her, he never could have hurt her. He could never hurt *any* woman.

"All right." The doctor squeezed Alena's hands once before turning and heading toward the doors. When she reached Andre, she paused, her gaze narrowed. "Don't upset her," she said tightly.

"I won't," he murmured. But he would get answers.

Then she was gone, leaving only Johnson. Andre could see it was against the man's instinct to leave but eventually he nodded at Alena. Then he looked at Andre, his expression hard. "I'll be out in the hallway. You've got five minutes."

Andre gritted his teeth but didn't respond. He didn't give a shit about this guy. All his focus was on Alena. He still hadn't wrapped his head around her being pregnant. Once the door shut behind Johnson, Andre crossed the distance to her. "Do you need to sit down?" he asked softly. Even if he had a whole lot of anger at her, he wasn't going to take it out on her now. She was vulnerable and he wasn't a monster. He wasn't like his father.

She looked vaguely surprised and nodded. "Actually yes, I will sit. I don't think I was ready for the big crowd and all those smells tonight. I got a little nauseous."

"How far along are you?" He knew she hadn't been with anyone for a long time before him—he'd checked that too. He didn't care if that made him a fucking stalker.

She glanced down at her clasped hands. "Sixteen weeks almost exactly."

"It's mine." A wave of possessiveness swept through him. And he wasn't going to analyze it right now. This woman simply brought out his protective instincts. Especially since he knew what his father had done to her family, how Yasha had left her and her sister orphans.

"Yes, it is. I was going to tell you, I swear."

He snorted at her words because he didn't believe anything she said. It was like a sucker punch to his solar plexus when she flinched, as if hurt.

But then her expression went completely neutral. "I deserved that. I assumed you would want to do a paternity test. I'm far enough along now that we can do a noninvasive one."

He shot to his feet and took a step back, reeling under the impact of her words. "Are you saying the baby might not be mine?"

She rolled her eyes, the picture of haughtiness— something he'd loved about her. "Of course it's yours," she snapped. "I just figured that you would want to do a test."

Relief rushed through him. "We'll do a test if you want, but I know that baby is mine."

She narrowed her eyes. "How could you know that?"

"Are you denying it?"

"No! I just assumed you'd want a paternity test, to make sure." She paused, gave him an uncertain look. "Have you been spying on me?"

"Yes." No need to deny it. He was who he was and didn't make apologies for it.

She blinked, clearly surprised by his bluntness. "Why?" she demanded.

"Because I fucking can." He wasn't going to give her a reason. Because he wasn't certain he actually had one. What was he going to say, that he was obsessed with her? That he couldn't get her out of his head? That even though she'd lied to him and literally tried to kill his father, he still wanted her more than his next breath.

She stared at him for a long moment, as if unsure what to say. Yeah, well, the feeling was mutual because he had no idea what to say either. He'd *thought* he'd known what he wanted to say to her tonight, but learning that she was pregnant had tilted his world on its axis. "If you're ready to leave, I can take you to your sister's house."

Nodding, she stood. Then she frowned, her spine stiffening. "How do you know I'm staying at my sister's?"

"Where else would you be staying? Because you're sure as hell not staying with Johnson. And you're definitely not going home with him."

Her back went even straighter as she took a step toward him. "You don't tell me what to do."

He gritted his teeth. He was used to giving orders and having things done immediately. He knew she wasn't one of his subordinates. And when they'd been together he hadn't treated her like one. But the thought of her going home with Nathaniel Johnson made him see red. Hell, the thought of her with any man made him crazy. Be civil, he ordered himself. He knew she wasn't with Johnson anyway. And he needed to stop acting like a jackass. "I would like to take you home and have a chance to speak with you in the privacy of my car." *There, that sounded civil.*

Her shoulders relaxed slightly and she nodded. God, in that shimmery dress, with her breasts all plumped up, he was having a hard time keeping his eyes on her face. Not when he wanted to bury his face between the mounds, tease her nipples until she was writhing underneath him, begging him to— *Nope.*

"I'll need to speak to Nathaniel," Alena said, "but yes, I would appreciate a ride home. I'd hate for him to have to miss this party because of me."

"May I..." He stopped at the last second, not sure how to ask the question.

"What?"

"It's hard to tell in your dress. I simply wanted to know if I could feel your stomach. But I don't want to overstep."

More than a touch of surprise flickered across her flawless features. As always, she was the vision of perfection and elegance. Dark eyes that missed nothing and a full mouth he had dreams about. She paused before nodding. "Yes, of course you can."

Even as he crossed the distance to her, he ached inside. He'd completely fallen for this woman. This beautiful little liar. And now she was carrying his baby. He wasn't sure how to digest that information, or what the hell he was going to do about it.

Slowly he reached out and cupped her belly, which was indeed a small bump. She must have chosen this dress specifically. Obviously. It covered the curve he felt, the roundness, but he imagined that when she was naked, the bump would be quite prominent. He immediately locked down thoughts of her naked, not wanting to go there. Now definitely wasn't the time. When he pulled his hand back, he felt...hell, he wasn't sure what he felt. Empty, lonely. Who the fuck knew?

"I need to speak to Nathaniel in the hallway without you being all, well, *Andre*. Do not threaten him." She gave him an annoyed look as he held the door open for her.

"Fine."

In the hallway he stood off to the side as Alena talked to the good-looking bastard in hushed tones. Johnson gave her a purse. Must have gone back to their table to get it for her. He didn't like what Alena was telling him, that much was clear in his tense body language, but he finally nodded and gave her a brief kiss on the forehead.

Andre hated it, but he let it go. Arguing or acting like a caveman wouldn't get him anywhere right now. Except... As a thought occurred to him, he pulled out his cell phone and texted his driver and his security for the night. He'd already told his security to stand down while he went to follow Alena—much to their annoyance. But he didn't care. Once he got a response, he turned back to see Johnson stalking away down the hallway, back to the party. Alena was going to be pissed about what he planned to do in the next few minutes but too damn bad.

"My car is waiting out front," he said, moving to Alena's side.

When she nodded, it was clear how tired she was. Not that anything took away from her beauty, but she seemed almost fragile. On instinct he wrapped his arm around her, wanting to make sure she was protected from any partygoers. He really must be a fool. He shouldn't be touching her. It was stupid. But he had this innate urge to keep her safe. "Use me to lean on if you need help walking."

"I think I'm fine now, but...thank you." She didn't wrap her arm around him, but even so, she fit perfectly against him as they headed toward the nearest set of doors.

Inside the ballroom, a man he'd done business with immediately started toward him, but Andre waved him off. Right now he simply wanted to get Alena to his car. The fastest way was straight through the gala.

Appearing as if from nowhere, his two security men for the evening moved in, one standing in front of them and another behind. He didn't think Alena was even aware of the men as they slowly made their way around the outskirts of the tables.

He hadn't thought about it before but the place was loud and there were a lot of rich scents filling the air.

He was aware of more than a few curious looks tossed their way, but he ignored all of them. Before Alena, he hadn't brought anyone to events. Just as he hadn't been seen in public with another woman for anything other than business. She was the first woman he'd been linked with since his wife's death a couple years ago.

And Alena had cut his heart out.

When they finally stepped outside, he was glad to see his limo parked right at the bottom of the red-carpeted stairs, his driver standing next to the back door.

"This is us," he murmured to her, holding her firmly as they descended the stairs. He was going to be making a very public claim on her soon.

As they reached the bottom, his driver opened the door. At the open door, she half turned into him, clearly ready to say something. He took the opportunity to lean down and brush his lips over hers. He knew it was a dick move, but he did everything with a purpose.

Even so, he should have been prepared for the reaction that jolted through him at the feel of her lips against his. She swayed into him for a fraction of a moment before pulling back, her expression shocked.

Her lips tightened with anger as she quickly ducked into the car. He slid in next to her. One of his security men got into the front seat with the driver and the other would be following behind them in another vehicle at a discreet distance. Now that his father was dead, security wasn't as intense. He'd been a target simply because of his criminal father, by people who hadn't particularly hated him, but who would have targeted Andre because of Yasha. He still kept some security though, because he did run a billion-dollar business.

"What the hell was that?" Her voice was breathy as the door shut behind them.

Lifting a shoulder and feigning a casualness he didn't feel, he said, "A picture of us should hit some kind of media site by tomorrow. Maybe even tonight. So when we get married, it won't be such a surprise. After all, we were linked together over four months ago."

"Married?"

Nodding, he pulled out his cell phone. No way would he be apart from the mother of his child. *My child.* This was happening. "It's the only thing that makes sense."

"Did you hit your freaking head? We're not getting married."

Turning to look at her, he wasn't surprised to see anger and hurt flicker across her face. "I'm going to be involved with my child's life every step of the way." Which meant he would live in the same damn house and be able to protect what was his.

"I'm not saying you can't be. Of course I want you to. But that has nothing to do with marriage. We'll figure something out. Couples do this all the time. So can we. As long as we're civil, maybe even one day friendly, I think...I'd be happy to co-parent with you." She looked so vulnerable in that moment. Before he could respond, she continued, "I know you probably have a lot to say to me. And probably are concerned about my skills as a mother."

He frowned at her words. He knew the things she had done. And he didn't judge—even if he was angry that she'd used him. He might not be exactly like his father, but he lived in shades of gray. She'd done what she had out of a sense of wanting justice. But he hated that he'd been a means to an end. That everything between them was an act. "I think you will be a fierce mother," he murmured, turning to look out the window.

She sucked in a surprised breath but didn't respond.

The bright colors and lights of Miami flew by as they headed down Ocean Drive. And when he turned to Alena again, her head was tilted back against the leather seat, her eyes closed and her breathing steady.

He couldn't believe she'd fallen asleep so quickly, but he was glad for it. After seeing Summer Freeman tonight he hoped that Alena wanted to use her while in Miami. The woman was one of the best. But he would research other OB/GYNs as well. His child would only get the best care.

Swallowing hard, he couldn't tear his gaze from Alena. She looked so peaceful, almost happy.

If he could go back in time…he would still want to have met her. He hated that she'd used him, even if he understood why she'd done it. And he couldn't say he was sad that she was pregnant. Surprised, yes. But he wasn't unhappy. As fucked up as it was—and he was well aware that he had his own issues—he liked being tied to her. More aptly, he liked that she was tied to him.

He never should have kicked her out of his life all those months ago. He should have known that he wouldn't be able to get over her. And he was done trying.

Alena was carrying his child and she would eventually be his wife. They weren't going to do some bullshit co-parenting thing where she might end up with someone else. Where some other man could help raise his child. Touch his woman.

Fuck. No.

He would do what was best for their child. His own father had been a monster. Andre wanted the chance to do this right.

CHAPTER FOUR

As the car pulled to a stop in her sister's driveway, Alena opened her eyes. For a moment, she looked confused before giving Andre an open, unguarded smile.

Just for a fleeting moment.

But then that guarded expression slid back into place. Not that he was surprised. Things were so screwed up between them. He wondered if they could ever make it right.

"I can't believe I fell asleep," Alena murmured, straightening her dress as she stretched, arching her back ever so slightly. Then she gave a short laugh. "It's not even ten o'clock. This really is sad."

"You're pregnant, it's natural you're tired. I'm sure you should be getting all the rest you want. Speaking of, how long will you be staying in Miami?" He needed to know so he could adjust his plans. He'd be sticking close to her. Even if they couldn't overcome the barriers between them right away, he was going to try.

"I'm not sure. I'm here to help out with Nika's wedding plans. They're getting married in a month and a half. I'll probably just stay until the wedding." She paused, eyed him warily. "I was actually thinking of moving here. It's close to my sister and I miss her. I think it would be good for me and…" She put a hand on her stomach but didn't continue.

He'd actually figured as much. "I have a place where you can stay. Actually, I have a handful to choose from. Condo or a house, whatever you prefer."

She shook her head. "No thanks, but I do appreciate the offer." Her words were stiff, but polite. "I'll likely find another place to stay for the next month and a half. My sister says I can stay here the whole time but I don't want to be a bad guest. And no one likes guests for longer than a few days."

He certainly wouldn't mind if she stayed with him indefinitely. The moment he had the thought, he frowned at himself. He would be insane to trust her, to let her into his life again. But she *was* in his life. And he wanted to try to make something real with her. Even as he told himself that he needed to keep walls between them, to keep his distance. He just wanted to marry her so their child could have a whole family, so that some other asshole wouldn't be raising his kid.

Yeah, he didn't think he could swallow his own lies.

Though he wanted to insist that she at least look at a couple of his places, he simply nodded. "The offer is always open. Also, I would like to set up a meeting with you and go over our co-parenting options, some things we should probably figure out. I can have my attorney set up a meeting with yours." He'd rather just figure things out themselves but thought it was what she would want.

"Do you really want to involve attorneys? I think we can figure out something just the two of us." She lifted her shoulder. "But whatever you want is fine with me."

Hell no, he didn't want to involve his attorney. Though he would mention it to the man because he'd have to make some changes, set up a new trust for his unborn child. "For now, I think the two of us can figure things out on our own. How do you feel about Dr. Freeman?"

"I really like her. And I'll need to find a doctor here in Miami for the duration of my stay whether it's just a month and a half or long-term."

"They do have great hospitals here." This entire conversation was so bizarre. He felt as if they were being ridiculously polite. But what was he going to do? Yell at her? He knew why she'd used him. He even understood it. If he'd been in her shoes he would have likely done the same thing.

She nodded. "Would you like to go to my first appointment with her? I'm sixteen weeks now, so in the second trimester. I should be coming up on another check-in soon anyway. My doctor in New Orleans has been seeing me every couple weeks like clockwork so I imagine it will be the same here."

He was glad she'd asked him, even if surprised. She'd only admitted that she was pregnant because she'd had no choice. He wanted to believe that she would have come to him, but who knew how long it would have taken her. Of course he would've found out on his own as soon as a pregnant picture of her hit the tabloids. He was surprised that Barry hadn't known about her visits to a doctor but Andre had only asked for certain details, like if she'd started seeing someone. "I'd like that. Also—" He paused, trying to find the right words so she wouldn't get annoyed. "I think you should take one of my security guys with you while you're here. I know you've had security in the past and I'm surprised you didn't have anyone with you tonight."

"I have basic security in New Orleans and usually when I travel for work, but I'm staying with my sister, and Declan has the most ridiculous security system."

"I'd still feel better."

"Are you actually asking?" She lifted an eyebrow. "You're usually so bossy."

"I'm trying to be civil." Because he simply couldn't be angry or yell at her, not when she was sitting here pregnant.

Some of the light dimmed from her gaze and he hated it. "Let me think on it," she finally said. "I'll set up an appointment with Summer next week. As soon as she can fit me in."

"I'd like to see you before then. What does your schedule look like tomorrow?"

"I'm going dress shopping with Nika. We're actually just going to one shop and trying on dresses. I can't believe she doesn't have her wedding dress picked out yet." Alena shook her head.

"Okay, what about tomorrow night? We can have dinner."

"Yes, that sounds good. And please no more talk of marriage." She rolled her eyes.

He definitely wasn't going to promise that. "I can pick you up wherever is easiest for you."

She nodded slowly, a small smile playing at her full lips. Lips he'd kissed, teased, nibbled on. "So far we really are off to a good start with this whole being-civil thing. I know that I said it the night..." She gave her head a little shake. "I'm not sorry for what I attempted to do to Yasha. But I am desperately sorry that I used you."

"Was anything we shared real?" Because the thought of her giving herself to him—sleeping with him when she didn't want to, just so she could get to his father—made him nauseous.

"It was, for me. I never expected to have feelings for you. At the time I actually wished that you were more like him. That you were at least a little bit horrible. It would have made it easier to use you. But you were the exact opposite of him, a good, decent man. And I really am so incredibly sorry for...using you."

He nodded, unable to find his voice. He had so many things he wanted to say to her, but couldn't force anything else out. Instead of responding, he opened the door and slid out, holding out a hand for her. She picked up her purse and took his hand. He wasn't surprised to see Declan waiting on the front porch, watching the two of them carefully. "Call me or text me tomorrow and we'll set up a time," he said to her.

She nodded, and for a moment it looked as if she might say something more but then she turned and headed toward the front door. She said something too low for him to hear to her brother-in-law-to-be before ducking inside.

Declan waited until the door shut behind her before striding toward him, a neutral expression on his face. Andre knew what the man was worth, and though the Coconut Grove home was nice, he was a little surprised he didn't live somewhere bigger, more upscale. Perhaps he shouldn't be. Everything about Declan Gallagher was understated.

They hadn't spoken much since four months ago, so Andre held out a hand. "Nice to see you."

Declan nodded once and took his hand. "You're bringing Alena home instead of her date?"

"He wasn't her fucking date." *Okay, way to remain civil.*

Declan just snorted. "I'm going to say this once. She told me that you know about her pregnancy. And I know what she did was wrong. But...not unwarranted. Regardless of what I think, Alena is Nika's sister. She loves her. If you hurt Alena in any way, I will hurt you." No drawn-out or explicit threats, just a simple truth from a dangerous man.

Andre was dangerous too. And he could respect Declan looking out for Alena. Was glad for it. "I would never hurt her. I couldn't." Even the thought of something happening to her— *No.*

Declan just gave him an assessing look, but didn't respond.

"Tomorrow it will likely hit the entertainment media that Alena and I are together, or at least have been seen kissing at the gala." Declan didn't seem surprised by this but the man was hard to read—try impossible. Andre continued. "I plan to be involved in her life and our child's life. And she's mine to protect now." He felt ridiculously possessive where she was concerned. It had been like that almost from the start. Maybe he should hold on to more anger but he couldn't find it in him. Not after seeing Alena in person again. She'd woven a spell over him.

Declan still didn't respond, just watched him. There was a reason the man had worked for the CIA. Something not many people knew. Andre guessed he'd been very good at his job.

"She won't take my offer of a place to stay while here in Miami, but I want her to at least take my security." He gritted his teeth, beyond frustrated that she even wanted to think about it.

"Have you offered her security?"

"Yes."

"Is there any particular reason you think she needs it?"

"She's pregnant." That was reason enough. Also, she was his.

"I'll subtly push her. And if she won't take yours, she'll take mine. I've already got a guy on standby to escort her and Nika anywhere they go if I'm not with them."

Right. Of course Declan would. "Okay, then."

Declan nodded and so did Andre. That was that. He headed back to his waiting vehicle, hating that he was heading home without Alena. Soon enough she wouldn't be separated from him. It was going to be a challenge convincing her they should be married but he was up to it.

"Are you crying again?" Eyes wide, Nika stared at Alena, hands on her hips.

In a stunning A-line wedding dress with an organza skirt and a long train decorated with thousands of beads and sequins, her sister looked lean, graceful, and ready to walk down the aisle. "I can't help it. My baby sister is getting married. And you look so beautiful in that dress. It's my favorite so far." Their mother would have loved to see Nika like this.

"You've literally said that about every single dress. And you started crying at over half of them. This is a whole new side of you."

Dabbing at her eyes, Alena nodded. "I know, it's ridiculous."

"It's not ridiculous, it's kind of sweet." Nika just shook her head, her lips curving up.

"Says no one but you. I'm going to look awful tonight when—"

"When what?"

"Ah, nothing."

Nika's gaze narrowed. "Spill it."

Alena hadn't mentioned to her sister that she'd be seeing Andre later. She had, of course, told her that Andre had brought her home last night and knew everything.

She was still reeling from seeing him in person, and all the feelings he evoked in her. Guilt and lust had been intertwined, fighting for dominance. And of course she couldn't forget her respect for him. Or...the L word. She wasn't going to think it. She *wasn't*. "I'm going to see Andre tonight. Not sure what time yet. He's supposed to text me later." It was already later afternoon and she was surprised he hadn't.

"I can't believe you didn't tell me. Was this meeting your idea or his?"

"Both. We're going to talk about the future for our baby, which feels way too surreal to say out loud." He'd been shockingly civil to her, which made her think that he could get past what she'd done. Maybe.

"With lawyers?"

"No. He mentioned it, but I really don't want to involve them. I feel like we could probably figure stuff out on our own." Of course that was only if things remained even-keeled between them.

"I think it's a good idea. And I'm glad he knows now."

Before Alena could respond, Tricia Brown, the owner of the shop, ducked her head behind the curtain of the dressing rooms. She smiled, her gaze going wide as she looked at Nika. "First, you look amazing. That one is definitely my favorite so far. Second, Declan is here."

Alena popped up from where she was stretched out on a tufted lounge chair. "You stay right here. He's not allowed to see you."

"Alena, that's ridiculous—"

"Nope. You're doing this one traditional thing." Her sister deserved to have some normalcy in her life. As maid of honor—and more importantly, as Nika's big sister—it was her job to make sure she did. "I'll take care of him."

The owner stepped into the dressing area and started talking to Nika about the dress.

Alena nearly ran into Declan as she rounded the corner. He was standing near a display of tiaras, looking a little uncomfortable in the store. And he wasn't alone. Her eyes widened when she saw Andre with him, his hands shoved into his pockets.

Today Andre had on black pants, a black Armani jacket—his favorite designer—and a blue shirt that matched his pale eyes. Of course he looked good enough to eat.

"What are you doing here?" she asked, looking between them, not sure who she was actually asking.

"I miss Nika," Declan said simply.

"Well you can't see her. Not now. She's still trying on dresses, and looks amazing in every single one." Oh God, she was going to start crying again like the overemotional wreck that she was.

Declan just smiled and took a step toward the curtain.

"Uh uh. I'm not messing around. It's bad luck." She gave his chest a light shove. "There's champagne over behind the checkout area. I'm sure Tricia wouldn't mind you getting some."

"Are you seriously dismissing me?" He looked amused by the very idea.

"You better believe it. I take this maid of honor business seriously. There will be no bad luck for you guys. Plus it'll be so much more meaningful if you don't see her in the dress until the big day."

Declan shook his head but did as she said.

When she turned to Andre she found him staring at her. "Wow," he murmured more to himself than her.

Seeing him again so soon was a punch to all her senses. She'd thought about him as she tried to fall asleep last night. Thought about, *fantasized* about...and even if it seemed crazy, she'd wished she'd never gotten out of that limo. Which was just plain stupid.

When she realized he was staring, she looked down at the formfitting navy-blue dress made of stretch lace. It was comfortable and actually looked good. And if she gained weight in the next month and a half—which she no doubt would—the middle part would stretch with her. It fell right to her knees, had a scoop neckline and detachable sash which secured at the empire waistline. It didn't look great hanging up, but Nika had insisted she try it on. And her sister had been right. As she often was. "You can really see the bump in this dress." *Way to state the obvious*, she mentally chided herself.

He stepped forward, quickly closing the distance between them. "Yeah." There was a touch of awe in his voice. When he met her gaze, he seemed to collect himself and that neutral expression was back in place. "Declan and I ran into each other at La Mar. He mentioned where he was heading so I figured I'd come with him. We can do an early dinner and talk once you're done here if you'd like?"

"That works for me." She knew her sister wouldn't mind, even if Alena was nervous about being alone with him again.

His gaze strayed down to her little bump again and she wasn't sure what to make of his expression. "A picture of us from last night surfaced online." He didn't sound sorry at all.

She took a step closer and lightly thumped him on the chest. "You can at least pretend to sound sorry."

He lifted a shoulder. "Why bother?"

She had no idea how to respond to that, or even his presence here. It was too jarring. And she still couldn't wrap her head around the fact that he thought they should get married. It obviously had nothing to do with any love for her. He was simply the type of man who wanted to do what his version of the right thing was.

But not her.

When she got married, it would be for love. She might have only been ten when her parents died, but she'd seen the real deal, and she wouldn't settle for anything less. She actually hadn't been sure it was even out there. Until Andre. But there was no way he could ever love her now. She couldn't even delude herself into thinking that. Could she marry him for the sake of their child? Hide her feelings for him for the rest of her life?

At the sound of the curtain being drawn back, she turned to find Nika stepping out in a light, flirty summer dress.

She was clearly surprised to see Andre but smiled at him. "Nice to see you."

He murmured the same even as Declan set down his still full champagne glass and crossed the short distance across the shop to Nika.

Alena watched them for a long moment together. One day she wanted what they had too. She was pretty sure that wasn't in the cards for her, however. She'd made her choices and she would live with them.

"If you want we can go somewhere public, show off your bump, then you can get the social media announcement out of the way. People will lose interest if you kill the speculation right away," Andre said.

She snorted even as she agreed with him. "You sound like my agent," she muttered. He was right, of course. "They're going to speculate about us too. So...are you going to make an announcement?"

"I'll have my assistant coordinate with your agent. Once we both approve the messages, they can go live."

"Okay." She let out a breathy laugh. "It's so ridiculous that we even have to do it." But it was something she'd learned to live with. It might be no one's business what she did with her life but it was one of those things that wasn't going away.

His lips curved up as humor lit those pale eyes. For a moment he was so relaxed and she had a flash of the first time they'd had sex on his desk. It had been hot, yes, but also fun. That had surprised her about him; he hadn't taken himself too seriously and he'd been so damn giving. He'd gone down on her, taken relish in it—had made things *all* about her. In her experience, the men she'd dated often only cared about having a model on their arm. She was just an accessory, something pretty to look at. With Andre, it was as if he'd seen her, had wanted to give her a ridiculous amount of pleasure because he *wanted* to. He'd ruined her for anyone else. Which seemed like a fitting punishment for her sins.

Sighing, she squashed all thoughts of sex and Andre. No need to go there. It would only leave her frustrated.

CHAPTER SIX

Andre watched Alena across the table from him at the popular seafood restaurant. The place was posh, and right on the Atlantic. He'd secured enough privacy for them that they were solo on one of the small balconies, but others inside the restaurant and from neighboring balconies could clearly see them. Which was just the way he'd planned it. He had something else planned, too, something he knew was going to piss her off.

He hadn't gotten to where he was by being passive. "Do you think we've had enough time in the public eye?" he asked, his gaze pinned to her.

She laughed and took a sip of her sparkling water. "I think we have. And I don't trust myself to eat too much here. I'm feeling okay now but I really don't want to get sick in public."

"Have you thought more about my marriage proposal?"

She kept her smile firmly in place, but he'd learned to differentiate between her fake and real ones. This one was very much fake. "You didn't propose." She let out a haughty little sniff. "And if I ever do get married, it will be after a real proposal. Not some lame business proposal. And that's exactly what you're proposing."

She was dead wrong. "I never said it would be just business between us."

Her gaze narrowed ever so slightly. "Of course that's all it would be. You'll never trust me." A hint of sadness crept into her eyes before she glanced away, looking out over the balcony.

Below them was a dance floor connected to the restaurant. It was early enough that there weren't that many people on it. But the tiki bar downstairs was busy, and there were people still on the beach even though it was after sunset.

"Oh look," she said, her eyes lighting up as a few fireworks started popping over the ocean. "We have a front row seat." A kaleidoscope of red, blue, green, and other colors exploded, lighting up the dark ocean below. She'd once told him that she loved fireworks.

As she watched, the delight in her expression so vivid, he felt a little guilty for what he was about to do. But not enough to stop. She was his, and he was going to do everything he could to keep her in his life and protect her. If that meant making her angry at him right now, he would take the risk and hope that it would work out in the end. He'd taken a lot of risks in his life, mostly business. She wasn't business though. Everything about Alena was personal.

His phone buzzed once, and without looking at the screen he knew what the message was. It was time. Reaching into his pocket, he pulled out the small red box and got down on one knee as the words *Marry Me Alena?* blasted across the sky in bright blue and green.

She sucked in a sharp breath and turned to find him kneeling in front of her. "What are you doing?"

"Giving you a proper proposal," he murmured, though it would be impossible for anyone to overhear them.

Her smile firmly in place—and a hint of panic in her eyes—she said, "We already decided against this."

"We didn't decide anything."

Reaching out, she cupped his face. He knew why she was doing it, because people were watching. That didn't mean he didn't like it. He did, very much. There was a glint of anger in her gaze. "You're very sneaky."

"You're one to talk."

"I can't say no to you, can I." It wasn't actually a question, just a realization on her part.

She *could* say no, but it would hit the entertainment media and give her the type of scrutiny she didn't want once her pregnancy came to light. Which was exactly why he'd done it. Yes, it was underhanded. He just didn't give a flying fuck.

When she didn't continue, he took her left hand and slid the engagement ring on her finger. "How's that for a proper proposal?"

Taking him by surprise, she leaned forward, took his face in her hands and crushed her mouth to his. It was the first time she'd ever been so bold. Before, he'd been the aggressor—and if he thought about that too long it would just anger him—so this was new. And not un-wanted. Kissing her back, he teased his tongue against hers, taking what she was offering until he forced him-self to pull away. There was only so much PDA he'd al-low the paparazzi or whomever to capture. His time with her was private.

But he'd needed to do this tonight. For a multitude of reasons. She was his and now everyone knew it.

Slightly dazed, she blinked at him. "I'm ready to go."

He nodded and stood. When she did the same, he pulled her tight to him, wrapping his arm around her as they stepped back into the restaurant. There were a handful of claps and a lot of congratulations tossed at them as they made their way through, his security flank-ing them from the front and back. Since he had a regular table here, he didn't need to bother paying. They simply billed the card he had on file and added a tip. It was one of the reasons he'd picked the place.

Once they were in the back seat of his car, he expected Alena to yell at him, but instead she curled up against the seat and gave him an assessing look.

"I should have expected that. In fact I'm surprised I didn't."

"I'm surprised you're not angry at me."

"I'm angry, but just because I said yes doesn't mean we're actually going to get married. We'll just let this play out in the media for a while. Because you and I are going to have a long engagement."

Yeah, he'd just see about that.

"Besides," she continued, "I'm too tired and too pregnant to be angry. The only reaction you'll probably get out of me is tears later."

Panic set in at that thought. Whatever was on his face made her giggle, a sound he'd never heard from her before. He liked it.

"I wish you could see your face," she said. "I'll try not to cry if it's going to freak you out. But no promises. This pregnancy is making me crazy." She yawned again.

Maybe so, but it was also making her even sexier. *Fuck.* She looked incredible and the knowledge that she was carrying *his* child did something strange to his insides. It made him feel even more possessive of her.

After a long moment of silence, she shifted in her seat, her body language changing slightly. He could see tension in her shoulders as she turned toward him. "How much did Declan tell you about...what happened to my parents?"

She knew that he'd seen pictures of the aftermath of their murder. A gory, bloody mess. He could only imagine how hard it was for her to bring up the subject. "He didn't tell me much. Just showed me the pictures and told me that they were from a classified file."

She flicked a glance to the front of the vehicle. The partition was firmly in place.

He answered her unspoken question. "My driver can't hear us."

Alena was silent for so long he didn't think she would continue. Then she said, "My parents were spies. And yes, this information is classified. But I'm not a spy and I don't work for the damn government. But...I'm going to trust you. Besides, you've earned this knowledge."

Her voice was quiet as she became silent again. Then she seemed to shake herself and continued.

"My mother was Russian and my father a British-American national. They were working for the Americans. My mother was truly an American by the time she was recruited by the CIA, but she'd been born in Russia. Anyway, they were apparently very good at what they did. According to my uncle they were both rule-breakers..." A sad smile flickered across her perfect features. "Even the two of them getting married in that time was bold."

He nodded, understanding what she meant. He'd seen a "before" picture of the couple. Her father had been a tall, ebony-skinned man and her mother white.

"But something went wrong, someone...found out and sent four men to kill them. Her, mainly. For being a traitor to her country. Your fath—Yasha was one of them. Nika and I were in the house when it happened."

He didn't respond or react outwardly, but inside, he raged against the man who'd been nothing more to him than a sperm donor. Andre certainly wasn't sad Yasha was dead. And he felt no guilt for betraying him to the government. Andre hoped that before Yasha died, he realized that Andre had betrayed him, that Andre was ultimately responsible for his death.

"Thanks to a relative, we were able to get out of the country and start over fresh in London. I won't give you those details yet. Maybe one day I will."

"I'm sorry," he said simply. Knowing *all* of the details now…it killed any residual anger he might have. Fuck. *Fuck.* He wanted to reach out and pull her to him, to hold her, but he wasn't sure she'd welcome his touch. He'd already pushed her enough for one night.

"I'm not telling you because I want you to feel sorry for me. Or even forgive me. I just thought you should know the details. You should know that the woman you claim to want to marry killed three men. Would have killed four, as you very well know. And I'm not sorry for it." He could see she wasn't, in the tense line of her jaw, the raw defiance in her gaze.

"I wouldn't believe you if you said you were. And I'm not judging you." His hands weren't squeaky clean either. "You're different than the woman I thought you were when I invited you to Miami."

She let out a dry laugh. "I know."

"I like this woman better." She wasn't a silly party girl, like she let the world believe. He hadn't thought she was when he'd met her. But he had thought she'd been a bit softer, sweeter. He liked this Alena.

If anything, she had a good head on her shoulders. Because yes, he'd looked into her when he'd decided to pursue a relationship with her. And she was very smart with her finances, didn't party like most people assumed, and hadn't taken many lovers. She was as selective as he was.

She blinked once, clearly surprised, then looked away and out the window.

"Did you find the peace you thought you would once you killed them?"

Alena turned to him again. "Yes. With Yasha and the others dead, I feel like I've been able to move on. That the world is a better place with them gone. I also know what I did was wrong. And if I ever have to pay for those crimes, so be it."

Yes, he liked this woman a *lot* better. Despite the lies she'd told him, despite using him, he could understand the choices she'd made. Some people saw the world in black and white, right and wrong. He wasn't one of those people.

"I'm glad you trusted me with this," he finally said.

Instead of responding, she scooted a little closer toward him. She didn't touch him, but she laid her head against the leather seat close to his and closed her eyes.

Within minutes, she was breathing steadily, clearly asleep. Sighing, he laid his own head back against the headrest. Then he rolled down the partition separating him and his driver, Juan.

"Change of plans. Head back to my estate." He'd originally told Juan that they would be making one stop, at her sister's place, before taking him home. But Andre wanted to push, to see how far he could get with her. Her admission—her honesty about her past—had ripped him open inside. Eventually he would convince her to move in with him. It was all about small steps.

* * *

Alena stood in the huge foyer of Andre's home. Estate was more like it. She'd stayed here with him months ago, and while it mostly looked the same, there were some changes. The interior was of course elegant, and she recognized some of the new art hanging as local Miami artists.

She should be annoyed at Andre for being presumptuous enough to bring her back to his house. And okay, she was annoyed, but she was tired more than anything. Plus if she stayed here, it gave Declan and Nika a night to themselves. Not that either of them had made her feel unwelcome, but she figured they would still like alone time.

While waiting for Andre to return from wherever he'd gone, she pulled her cell phone out of her purse. There was only one person she wanted to call. Actually, two. Because she definitely needed to call her agent and give her a heads-up. But first, she dialed her sister.

"Hey, I thought you'd be home earlier. Everything okay?" Nika asked, picking up on the second ring.

"Everything's fine. But I'm going to be staying at Andre's tonight. In a guestroom," she tacked on.

"Hmm, is that right?" There was a tone in her sister's voice she couldn't quite read.

"Yes, that is right."

"Then what's this I hear about you two being engaged?"

Sighing, she stepped into a formal sitting room right off the foyer. Slipping off her heels, she sat on one of the leather chesterfields by the window. A sea of rich green grass and palm trees illuminated by the moonlight and security lights stretched out in front of her. "Wow, news travels fast." And she really needed to call her agent.

"Declan got a call from someone he knew who was at the restaurant."

"We're not engaged. He proposed because he's being a stubborn jackass. He seems to think that since I'm pregnant, we should get married. Which is just ridiculous."

"Hmm."

"What's up with these cryptic little *hmm* sounds?"

"I just think it's probably not the only reason he wants to be with you."

"I'm not getting into that now." Yes, she knew Andre was attracted to her. But the thought of getting married for that and their child was insane.

"Fine, but I think you're only fooling yourself."

Closing her eyes, she let her head fall back against the leather seat. She wasn't fooling herself. Andre was a man used to getting what he wanted. He was trying to be in control right now for whatever reason. But there was no way they could ever get married. It was pure insanity. He would never trust her. But they could work on their relationship. They already had the civil part down pat. It was easy to be civil with him because he really was a good person, if a bit of a bulldozer. And she had no doubt that he would be a good father.

On an intellectual level she knew she would be a good mother, too, but the thought was still terrifying. She knew nothing about children or babies. "Did we have any plans for tomorrow?" She didn't think they did, but wanted to be sure.

"Nope. No wedding stuff on the agenda. I actually have an appointment with a detective friend of mine tomorrow morning and I don't know how long I'll be. So don't feel like you have to rush back tomorrow."

"Okay. Also, you guys are wonderful but I don't want to overstay my welcome since I'm going to be here until your wedding. So I'll probably start looking for a place very close to you soon. I want to be involved in everything wedding related but I don't want to cramp your style."

Nika laughed lightly. "If you were anyone else, I would say that three days was enough and you should be gone. But it's you. You could stay as long as you want. I understand wanting privacy, however. I'm sure Declan knows a local Realtor who can help you find a place to rent. One of those corporate, fully furnished ones. Unless you want to start looking to buy?" There was a note of hope in her sister's voice.

"Definitely just looking to rent right now," she said, laughing.

"So...what does the ring look like?"

"Oh my God, you can't be serious?"

"I'm totally serious. Also, did he actually ask you with fireworks?"

She glanced down at her ring finger—while telling herself to take the damn thing off—and admired it. It was hard not to stare. The single princess-cut diamond was flawless and had to be at least three carats. "It's gorgeous." Not that she would expect anything less from a man like Andre Makarov. "And yes, yes he did. Sneaky man."

"It's pretty romantic," Nika said.

"It's..." She wasn't going to get into a whole thing with her sister about how it wasn't romantic, it was just a calculated decision on his part. Or at least she was pretty sure it was. He was a powerful businessman used to getting what he wanted. "Did you enjoy the alone time with your man tonight?" she asked, deciding to change topics.

"I know you're trying to distract me, and yes we did."

"So what's this meeting about that you have tomorrow? Or can you not tell me?"

"I don't actually know at this point."

Alena was starting to respond when she heard the faint sound of footsteps. "I think I hear Andre, so I'm going to get off the phone. But I'll text you tomorrow with my plans. I'll probably be at your place by tomorrow afternoon."

"Sounds good. Love you."

"Love you too." She glanced at the entryway as Andre stepped inside, looking good enough to eat.

He'd shed his jacket but was still wearing the same Armani slacks and button-down shirt. The luxury clothing didn't take away from his edge, from the toned, powerful body she knew was under all the clothing. "Is your sister worried I kidnapped you?"

She wasn't surprised that he realized she'd been talking to her sister. "No." She started to tell him that Nika wasn't even surprised she was here but held back. "I should be mad at you." Why wasn't she mad at him, dammit?

As he strode toward her, he reminded her of a sleek tiger. He sat on the other end of the chesterfield, all strength and sexiness. She wanted to lean over and nibble on his bottom lip.

"I'm surprised you're not," he murmured.

"Like I said in your car, I think I'm just too pregnant and too tired to be angry at anything."

"So, if I said we should get married in Vegas tomorrow—"

"Not that tired or pregnant. Seriously, Andre..." She looked down at the ring, shook her head. "It is gorgeous. And you know you've just given my agent a heart attack. I still need to call her."

He shrugged, not looking the least bit apologetic. "How are you feeling? Any nausea?"

She knew he was just trying to change the subject and that was fine for now. "No. I'm pretty good. Supposedly more into the second trimester the nausea is supposed to abate, but we will see." She stretched out slightly on the couch. "I could fall asleep on this thing."

Laughing, he took one of her feet in his big hands—then froze. He'd seemed to do it without thinking, clearly. "I was..." He let her foot go.

That one little touch practically set her nerves on fire. Which was ridiculous. One touch shouldn't have that effect on her. But it did. Because she remembered how talented he was with those hands.

He abruptly stood. "I have a guest room ready for you if you're tired. And some of the clothes you left before... They're still here. Though I don't know if they'll fit."

"I'm sure whatever is here is fine." Feeling awkward, she stood. As she did, a wave of nausea swept through her. *Oh no.* Without saying a word to him, she ran from the room, her bare feet slapping against the marble and then wood floor. So much for feeling fine. When she reached the nearest hallway she remembered the layout of his house just fine.

Throwing the guest bathroom door open, she plunged inside just in time to empty the contents of her stomach in the toilet. As she finished, a big hand landed in the middle of her back, making her jump and then cringe in embarrassment.

Of course he'd followed her. Shutting the lid, she flushed and started to stand, but he gently took one of her elbows and helped her. Without looking at him, she rinsed out her mouth and splashed water on her face, which helped her feel more normal.

Finally she met his gaze in the mirror. He was frowning at her. "If you feel embarrassed, stop right now." Then he opened a drawer and pulled out a small travel toothbrush and toothpaste kit. Moving quickly, he opened the package and handed them to her. As she brushed her teeth, he continued. "I'm sorry you're getting sick. I wish there was something I could do. Do you think I should call Dr. Freeman?"

The concern she saw on his expression in the mirror made her start crying. *Because right now couldn't get any more awkward*, she thought wryly. She spit out the toothpaste and rinsed her mouth before wiping away her tears.

"That's it, I'm calling the doctor."

Shaking her head, she let out a weak laugh as her tears dried up. "No. That's not necessary. I wasn't kidding about being emotional. You looked so concerned and I don't know, I just started crying."

Reaching out, he cupped her cheek gently, swiping at a stray tear. She wanted to close her eyes, to lean into his touch and the feel of his faintly callused fingers. But only madness lay down that path.

She was just being emotional tonight, that was all. At least that was what she told herself. Clearing her throat, she took a small step back and looked down at her clasped hands. "I think I'm ready to get some rest," she murmured. *Liar, liar.*

After a moment he made a sort of grunting sound and indicated that she should follow him. Tomorrow would be a new day. She would be stronger, more rested, and be able to get some distance from him. Some distance from all these feelings that he evoked inside her. Then she had to figure out a way to get over him. Which seemed impossible, considering they were now tied together. But she didn't want him to be with her for the reason he'd come up with. Obligation, whatever, it didn't matter. She wasn't going to settle for being his obligation.

CHAPTER SEVEN

Alena woke up feeling more refreshed than she could remember being in months. Which made no sense. She was in Andre's house, a place that held bad memories. Although it held good memories as well. Super sexy, *delicious* memories.

At that thought, a rush of heat pooled between her legs. Which wasn't exactly a surprise. Ever since he'd walked back into her orbit, her libido had flared to life.

Shaking that thought off, she got out of bed and made her way to the luxury bathroom. No nausea, which was good. After a quick shower, she looked inside the walk-in closet and found a handful of clothes from the last time she'd been here. After the insanity of that last night, when she'd attempted to kill Andre's father, she hadn't been in her right state of mind. Later she'd realized that she left some of her things behind, but hadn't even thought to ask Andre for them. They were just clothes. And she'd known he wouldn't want to talk to or see her.

She was surprised that he'd kept her things. She wasn't going to overanalyze why he might have either. More likely than not, he'd simply left his Miami estate and forgotten about them. The jeans were too tight but she found a pair of black leggings and a flowing top that had been loose before. Now it pulled across her baby bump snugly, but the ensemble looked cute.

With her hair left down in natural waves and no makeup, she was different than the sexy vixen who'd stayed here before. But this was the real her. Not the made-up woman on billboards and magazine ads. That was just her job. One she appreciated. And she did love fashion. But she didn't like to be "on" all the time. She wondered what Andre would think of the real her, and simultaneously hated that she even cared. But it was hard not to. Because she did care what he thought. She cared about *him*. Which was why it had been so hard seeing him, why she felt insane for even being at his house—and "engaged" to him. She wasn't sure what the hell she was going to do about *that* either.

When she stepped out of the bedroom, there was no one waiting. No guards. So different than the last time she'd been there. He'd had extra threats then and his father had still been alive. She'd heard from her sister via Declan that Andre had decreased his security since Yasha's death. The man had posed a threat to Andre simply by being alive. Because he'd had so many damn enemies. She being one of them. Something she didn't want to think about right now. That dead man had no right to take up space in her brain.

The marble was cold beneath her feet as she stepped into the foyer. Through the glass panes in the front doors she could make out a couple guards standing out front. She thought of heading to Andre's office to find him but decided to hit the kitchen first. She might not be allowed to drink regular coffee but she hoped he had decaf.

Glancing around the Mediterranean-style room, she saw that everything was just as she remembered. Braids of garlic and other spices hung from the iron pot rack over the marble-topped center island. And, more importantly than anything, there was a Keurig.

Next to it, little coffee pods were in a nickel-plated carousel—including decaf. She pulled one out as she turned on the coffee machine to heat the water, then found the biggest mug in the cabinet. When it started brewing, she inhaled the rich scent. Other than being nauseous all the time, not being able to have regular coffee was the only thing she hated about her pregnancy so far. Everything else was kind of wonderful, if a little terrifying.

Once it was done brewing, she picked up her mug and sat at the circular mosaic table in the small breakfast nook. The blinds were pulled up, giving her a perfect view of the glistening pool and lanai. When she saw Andre step outside onto the lanai with a tall brunette woman—wearing a tiny bikini—she frowned. They were standing very close to each other, but the woman's back was to Alena. And the woman looked good, all sleek lines and muscle.

Only half of Andre's face was visible, but he was smiling as he spoke to the woman, his hands shoved into his pockets, his expression easy and open. Alena squashed the irrational jealousy that bubbled up inside her. He could talk to whoever he wanted. He could *do* whatever he wanted. This was his house and they weren't together. Not really. Okay, not at all.

Last night she'd been pretty sure that if she'd attempted to kiss him he wouldn't have rejected her. But now...she wondered.

Feeling as if she was spying on him, she slid out of her seat, picking her mug up with her. As she did he leaned forward and kissed the woman on her forehead. It was an affectionate gesture, and that jealousy inside her went haywire. Who was this woman at his house—at nine o'clock in the morning? Wearing a skimpy bathing suit, no less. She clearly didn't work for Andre, so why else could she be here other than for him? Had she stayed in his bed last night? The thought made Alena feel sick.

Turning away, Alena left, making her way upstairs. She so did not need to see any of that. Nope, she was going to get her stuff and leave. She never should have stayed last night anyway. It had been foolish and clearly she wasn't thinking straight.

After folding all of her clothes neatly on the bed she froze at the sound of a knock on her door. "Come in," she called out.

Andre stepped inside, a tentative smile on his face. Though he frowned at her folded clothes. "How did you sleep?"

She wanted to ask him about the woman downstairs and how *he'd* slept, but kept the question to herself. He hadn't seen her in the kitchen and she wasn't going to tell him. She didn't want to come off as jealous. "Wonderful, thank you. I'm probably going to go ahead and get out of here soon. I have some errands to take care of today."

"I can take you." He leaned against the doorframe, watching her with an intensity that made her feel vulnerable, completely bare in front of him. Damn him.

"That's not necessary." Being around him was wreaking havoc on her already frayed nerves. "But I appreciate the offer," she added.

He pushed up from the doorframe. "What kind of errands do you have to do?" There was a tone in his voice she wasn't sure she liked.

"None of your business," she said, frowning at him. He obviously didn't tell her everything he did, and she wasn't going to start telling him. Because they didn't have a relationship, no matter what he was trying to create between them.

"You're upset about something." He took a step into the bedroom.

"No, I'm not."

"Are you really going to stand there and lie to me?"

"I'm pregnant. I'm allowed to be emotional and irrational anytime I want," she tossed out. Especially since he'd proposed. But she knew that was just a business thing for him. Even as she said the words she felt crazy. It was impossible to describe the emotions running rampant inside her and deep down she knew she couldn't blame them all on her pregnancy. She hated seeing him with another woman, yes, but it wasn't as if he'd been making out with the woman. No, Alena was upset with herself and how she felt being around Andre.

Out of control, vulnerable, guilty, and yes, turned on. That was the most ridiculous thing of all. Maybe not so ridiculous but right now she simply couldn't deal with being around him.

He paused for a long moment then nodded. "Have you rented a car yet?"

"No, I haven't gotten that far. Declan offered to let me use one of his company vehicles anyway."

"Take one of mine. I have half a dozen in Miami. I'll feel better knowing you're in a sturdy, safe vehicle." That protective note was back in his voice.

And she could admit that she liked his protectiveness. Even if it wasn't actually for her, but their unborn baby instead. There was no reason to argue with him. "Are you sure?"

He made a dismissive sound then nodded at the clothes. "You can just leave them here if you'd like."

"Most of these don't fit anyway." And she didn't plan on leaving her things here. That would indicate she would be coming back. And she wasn't sure that she would. She wasn't sure about anything right now.

He paused again, still watching her with that painful intensity, making her want to squirm. "Are you sure there isn't something you want to talk about?"

She was seriously tempted to ask him about the woman she'd seen downstairs but held back in case she hated his answer. "No."

He nodded and picked up her clothes for her. Downstairs, he had one of his men bring around a Land Rover. "Would you have dinner with me again tonight?" he asked as he walked her to the open driver's side door. He was all politeness and civility. Something she should like. But for some reason, it grated on her nerves.

"I'm not sure what Nika has planned tonight, but I'll let you know."

"That sounds a lot like a no."

"It's not like we have to prove a point anyway. We made a big splash last night."

"I'm asking you to have dinner here," he said quietly.

Oh. She bit her bottom lip, contemplating. "I'll let you know."

He nodded once, and to her utmost surprise, leaned down and brushed his lips over hers. When he pulled back there was a predatory gleam in his eyes, the heat there unmistakable.

She had no idea what to say, but in that moment she knew she needed to leave. She mumbled a half-assed thanks for the vehicle and slid behind the wheel. Once she was on the road, she knew she wasn't going back to Nika's. Her sister had said she wouldn't be there today and Alena didn't want to be alone right now. She had a few friends in Miami, but there was one friend she needed to talk to anyway. Especially after her "engagement" story had already hit the media. It wasn't as if it was front-page news, nor second or third, but some of her friends would have seen it by now.

Especially Nathaniel. She wasn't going to tell him the engagement was fake, but she did want to talk to him in person. Especially after the way she'd left the party the other night.

Then...she needed to sit down and talk to Andre. But first she needed to get her emotions in check. She couldn't have a breakdown in front of him and start crying. No, she needed to figure out what she wanted to say—like asking him about that woman—and then just get it all out there.

CHAPTER EIGHT

"You're really engaged now?" Nathaniel asked as he brought her a bottle of water.

On the balcony of his beachfront condo, Alena glanced out at the Atlantic before turning back to him. The salty tinge of the ocean in the air was refreshing and she hadn't felt nauseous all morning. "It would seem so." And she was still wearing the ring Andre had given her. It was simply to maintain cover, she told herself. She could almost buy her own lie.

"He's a very successful man. Also dangerous. Do you know who his father was?"

Alena held back a snort. She might be friends with Nathaniel, but there were some things none of her friends would ever know about her. Not the name she'd been given when she was born, and not what had truly happened to her parents. The little girl she'd been then was dead. She didn't even think of herself by that name. She was Alena. "Yes. I know who he was. He shouldn't be judged by that."

Nathaniel lifted a big shoulder. "Does he treat you well?"

"Yes. Things between us are complicated though." And that was all she planned to say about that. "How was the rest of the gala Saturday?"

He cleared his throat, giving her a wicked smile. "My night ended well."

She lifted an eyebrow. "Oh really?"

"Yes."

"You can't leave me hanging like that. Who did you hook up with?" Because a smile like that meant only one thing.

"It's more than a hookup... I'm dating Summer Freeman now. I really like her."

Alena grinned. "I can definitely see that. There always seemed to be a spark between the two of you."

"She was always with someone at these stupid events. I didn't realize she was single," he grumbled.

"You're always with someone at events like that—often with me. She probably didn't realize you were single either."

He let out a bark of laughter. "That's exactly what she said. She thought we were an item until Andre showed up."

Just the mention of Andre's name had her shifting slightly in her seat. She wondered if he was with that woman right now, then cursed the stupid thought. She started to change the subject, then Nathaniel glanced down at his phone.

"Hold on, that's the front desk."

She half listened to his one-sided conversation, which was mainly just grunts, and looked out at the ocean. There were jet skiers, boaters, and hundreds of people sunbathing on the beautiful white sand. The weather was perfect, and with the cool breeze blowing over her, the only thing that would make it better would be if she could actually dip her toes in the sand.

"Excuse me for a moment," Nathaniel said, rising from his chair.

She nodded and picked up her bottle of water as he stepped back into his condo. A few moments later, she heard Andre's very annoyed voice. Turning, she found him and Nathaniel striding out onto the balcony. Surprise ricocheted through her.

"What are you doing here?" Water bottle still in hand, she stood, concerned. Was something wrong? How had he even known she was here?

"What the hell are you doing here?" he snapped.

His tone made her straighten. Nathaniel still stood in the doorway, his expression neutral, but he didn't seem overly pissed off. Which surprised her. "Tell her why you're here," Nathaniel said dryly. "Instead of being a dick."

"Yes, tell me why you're here."

"You said you had errands to run today," Andre said, still not answering her question. And there was an accusatory tone in his voice.

Suddenly it hit her... "Oh my God, is there some kind of GPS tracker in your vehicle?"

He shrugged. "All my vehicles have that, and yes, that's how I knew you were here."

He would have had to have done some sort of search on the owners or occupants at this condominium and then narrowed down which unit she was at. She didn't call him out on that. Instead she set her bottle down and placed her hands on her hips. "That's insane."

Again, he shrugged. Which just infuriated her more. He was so unapologetic about his behavior. "You didn't answer your phone. And I got a call from Declan, worried about you."

All of her annoyance bled out of her in an instant. She covered the distance between them, her heart racing. "Is my sister okay?"

"Yes, of course. She's fine. Both she and Declan are." The relief that slid through her was intense, until he said, "But...Harold Brady is out of prison. A couple hours ago there was a riot at the prison, and five inmates escaped. Three were found in the first two hours but two are still missing. Including Brady."

Feeling the blood drain from her face, Alena sat back down. Andre shouldn't even know that name. She'd never brought Brady up to him. But he did, so Declan or Nika must have told him about it. "There's no way he could be here, in Miami." Harold Brady was in a maximum-security prison up in New York, so even if he knew where she was there was no way he would be able to make it down to Miami in a couple hours. Nonetheless, that panic was back.

Brady had stalked her, but that wasn't what landed him in jail. He'd killed three people—shot them point blank in the head—in his insane effort to win her affection. Over the years she'd had enough stalkers and weirdos that were harmless enough, but Brady had been batshit crazy. She knew that wasn't the legal term and she didn't care—he was. She'd never had much interaction with him, and he'd never actually hurt her, but the letters he'd sent her had been disturbing. And he'd sworn he would get out of jail. And that when he did he would "make her his" because he knew they belonged together.

It had just hit the media that she and Andre were engaged—and she was clearly pregnant, even if they hadn't made the official announcement yet. "I don't want to be anywhere near my sister or Declan," she said. She had no doubt that Declan could protect Nika. And being around her sister would just make Nika a target if Brady ever made it down to Miami. She hoped that he wouldn't, that the police would catch him and put him right back where he belonged.

"You'll stay with me. And if they don't catch him soon, I'm taking you to Vegas. My estate there is beyond secure."

On shaky legs, she stood. They could talk about future plans later, but for now she needed to leave with Andre. Turning to Nathaniel, she gave him a wry smile to cover her anxiety. "Apparently I'm just full of drama lately."

Laughing lightly, he shook his head and pulled her into a hug. Behind her, it almost sounded like Andre growled, but that was ridiculous. As she stepped back from Nathaniel, he gave Andre a hard look.

"You better keep her safe."

"I don't need you to tell me that." Andre placed a gentle but firm hand at the small of her back as he led her back through the condo. Before she could say anything, he picked up her purse from the counter in the kitchen on their way out.

And apparently that was that.

* * *

Andre tried to keep his annoyance in check as they made their way down the elevator and to his waiting vehicle. Once he had Alena safely in the passenger seat of his vehicle and was steering out of the parking garage, the leash on his temper snapped.

"Why the hell were you at Johnson's place?" He barely kept the growl out of his voice.

Or not at all, if the way she stiffened was any indication. "I thought we decided to be civil. And you don't get to be annoyed at me for going over to a friend's house."

"Have you ever fucked him?" he demanded. Inwardly he winced at his snarly tone.

"Oh, you have a lot of nerve!" She turned away from him, looking out the window.

"That's not an answer."

Letting out an exasperated sound, she turned to him. "No. Not that it's any of your business. And I don't like this side of you!"

"Yeah, well too bad. I don't want you going over to his place without me. Or any man's place." He knew he sounded like a jackass but couldn't seem to stop himself.

She stared at him, her dark eyes wide.

He glanced at the light. Still red. "This can't be a shock to you." His voice was dry. How could she not realize how much she still made him crazy? How much he still wanted her? How he wanted her right fucking now?

"Is this...you being jealous?" There was a note of hesitation in her voice.

No sense in denying it. "Yes."

"That's really rich," she snapped. "Especially since you had some random woman at your house this morning—with me there." Fire sparked in her eyes. "Oh yeah," she said before he could respond. "I saw you kissing her out by your pool, so save your bullshit jealousy routine."

That surprised him. "You care if I kiss another woman?"

To his utter horror she started crying again.

"Damn it!" she snarled, more at herself, he thought, than him. "These tears aren't because of you, so don't flatter yourself!" She turned away again, crossing her arms over her chest. "Stupid hormones."

Guilt filtered through him. He should have just told her right away. "The person you saw this morning is my sister. And if you were watching, then you saw me kiss her on the *forehead*. She stopped by unexpectedly and wanted to meet you, especially after that media announcement." He could have kicked himself for not telling Kiley before she'd seen it on the news. But he'd been so focused on his plan to convince Alena to marry him, he hadn't thought of anyone else.

Alena turned to him again as they pulled up to another red light, her expression still wary. "Your sister has blonde hair."

"She changes her hair color every other month. This month it's brown."

"Oh...I thought she lived in Vegas."

"She does. She's in town for business."

"Oh." She bit her bottom lip, her cheeks turning the sexiest shade of red.

His blood heated at the sight and, making a snap decision, he took a left at the next turnoff, stopping in a Publix parking lot. "You were jealous at the thought of me and another woman?"

"Yes. I know I have no right to ask, but I had wondered if you'd been with anyone since..." She bit her bottom lip again.

"No." He didn't want anyone but her.

"I haven't either. Been with a man, I mean. Or a woman either, obviously...I'm rambling."

Reaching out slowly, giving her time to tell him to stop, he cupped her cheek. He missed touching her.

Eyes heavy-lidded, she whispered, "What are you doing?"

"Nothing right now. But when we get back to my place I want to get you naked." There. Might as well get it right out in the open. He didn't want there to be any confusion about what he wanted. And that was her.

"How could you want me and hate me at the same time?"

"I don't hate you." He leaned his forehead against hers, closed his eyes for a moment before pulling back and dropping his hand. "I hated my father. Almost as much as you hated him. And...I understand why you used me. I hate that you did, but I don't think I could ever hate you." He turned back in his seat and stared blindly out the windshield.

"So...what do you want from me?"

"I don't think you want the answer to that."

"I do."

"I want the real you. I got some of it before. And I'm starting to see more of it now. I like the fiery Alena, the one who yells at me. And...I want to ask you... When you slept with me—"

"I wanted to." Surprising him, she took his hand, linked her fingers through his. "More than I should have," she murmured. "So if you ever worried that...if you thought I didn't want to, I did. Very much. It never occurred to me to tell you afterward because I assumed you knew how much I wanted you."

Relief slid through him. When he looked at her again, her cheeks were that sexy crimson. "Yeah?"

"Yes. And if you want more of the real me, then the woman who sat by and let a man call her a whore at your dining room table...that's not me. If it had been any other circumstances, I would have tossed a drink in Yasha's face and slapped him. And probably had some choice words for him, but more likely his face would have met my palm."

"Or his trachea would have met your fist."

She let out an unexpected laugh at his reference to what she'd had to do to someone once months before. That seemed like a lifetime ago. "Or that... My uncle, the man who raised me, he taught both Nika and me self-defense. And I've kept up with it."

With the amount of weirdos he imagined she dealt with, it made him happy she could take care of herself. But that brought him back to... "We need to talk about Brady." And what they were going to do if the man wasn't caught.

Sighing, she slumped back in her seat. "Yeah, I know."

He pulled out of the parking lot. It was time to get Alena back to his place. If he had to keep her locked down to make sure she was safe, so be it. Staying under the same roof with her was certainly no hardship. He planned to keep her there, even after Brady was caught.

CHAPTER NINE

Alena ended her phone call with her agent and before she'd put it down on the table next to her lounge chair, it rang again. Nika. "Hey," she answered. Stretching out under the deck umbrella, she savored the view of the sparkling pool water and the light breeze.

"I would have called you back sooner but I was waiting for Declan to get off the phone with Andre. I don't have anything new for you though. How are you holding up?"

"Honestly, I'm fine. The police are going to find Brady. It's not like he's some evil genius." He was crazy, yes, but he'd killed three people and hadn't hidden the bodies, hadn't made an attempt to cover his tracks, nothing. The man lived in an alternate reality where he thought they belonged together and other people were simply keeping her from him. She just hoped the police found him before he hurt anyone.

"Come on, you can be honest with me."

"I'm serious. If he's not found in a few days I'll probably start worrying a bit. But I'm going to be smart, and stay locked down here for a while. Have you...had any visions?" For all her psychic gifts, Nika almost never had any visions about those closest to her. It had only happened once and it had been so brief—and they'd interpreted it wrong.

"No, unfortunately. Not that I really expected to have one." Frustration laced Nika's voice.

"Is there any wedding stuff I should be helping out with right now?"

"Don't change the subject."

"I'm not. There's literally nothing I can do right now about Brady."

"Uh, yeah there is. You can stay put where you're safe. And if you need to leave, for whatever reason, you can either come back to our place or Declan said he'll set you up in a safe house."

"Thank him for his concern, but I think I'm fine for now. I also think..." She glanced over her shoulder to the sliding glass doors. All of the windows and doors had a tint on them so it was impossible to see inside. But she was definitely alone on the lanai. "I think maybe something might be happening with Andre."

"What do you mean?"

"Ah...never mind." Gah, why was she even talking about this?

"Wait, you mean between the two of you?"

"No. Maybe. Yes...I think. Damn it, I don't know. Maybe I'm crazy to even be thinking of this."

"Uh, no." Her sister's voice was dry. "You were into him even when... Well, you know. And I don't think you ever got over him. Tell me I'm wrong."

"I can't," Alena whispered.

"Exactly. So…make a move on him."

"What?" That wasn't her style. Not even a little bit. She could admit she liked being pursued. But…this was different.

"You hurt him. You have to make the first move."

"What if he doesn't want me?" What if it was just lust for Andre? And that was the real crux of her issue. Because lust would fade. And she was in love with him. Big difference.

"Then you deal with it… But the man proposed to you. I'm pretty sure he wants you."

"He proposed because… Damn it, Nika. When did you get to be so smart?" She couldn't find the words to admit her deepest fear: that this was just about lust and control for Andre.

"I'm a genius. About time you recognized it."

She snorted softly as laughter bubbled up inside her. "God, I've missed seeing you every day."

"I know. Me too. The phone is good, but in person is a lot better."

"Would it be too weird if I asked you and Declan to come over here for dinner one night? If Brady hasn't been found yet?" Something she didn't even want to think about. She'd come to Miami to see her sister and spend time with her. Alena didn't want to be separated from Nika because of a madman.

"If Andre is fine with it, then we'll be there."

"Okay, I'll talk to him." She couldn't imagine that he would mind.

"Why don't you talk to him when you're naked." Nika snickered.

"Oh my God, hush. Also...I'm pregnant. What if—"

"Stop right there. He won't care if your body is different. If anything, he'll love it. He put a baby in you. It's a total caveman thing."

"Seriously?"

"Yes. I'm getting married to a caveman, so I know."

"Are you guys talking about having kids?"

"Ah...not right after the wedding or anything. But yeah, we've talked." She could practically hear the smile in her sister's voice.

"Hurry up, then. We can be stroller buddies." Words she never thought she'd say. So much of her life had been about her job, and then revenge. It had consumed her to the point where she hadn't been willing to listen to reason. Hadn't been willing to listen even to her sister. Alena was lucky that she and Nika were alive. Because if she'd lost her sister because of her own blind need for revenge, she wasn't sure she could have lived with that.

"Eh, maybe not quite that soon. Yours might be in kindergarten by the time we start."

"Whatever works for you guys. All right...I think I'm going to put myself out there with Andre."

"Good. Do it now."

"He's working." He'd told her that he'd be in his office for a while.

"So? I love interrupting Declan at his office." Nika snickered again.

"All right, I so do not want those details. Not now anyway."

"Prude."

She laughed and when they finally ended their call, she felt lighter than she had in months. Her sister was right. She needed to put herself out there. If Andre rejected her, then so be it. It would probably be awkward for a while but that was a risk she was willing to take.

Pushing up from the lounge chair, she saw a slight movement from the wall surrounding the back of his property. For a moment, panic set in but then she recognized one of his security guys. Of course, she knew there were people patrolling the property. They were just really good at blending in.

No more excuses. It was time to make a move.

* * *

"I'm done with this conversation," Andre said for the second time to Roger Thatcher, one of his attorneys.

"I'm just saying, I've drawn up a sample for you. You can use it as a guideline when working out a schedule with her. Don't be stupid. People talk about being civil all the time and then shit goes sideways. You need something in place to protect your assets. And she needs something too. This isn't about me not trusting her. I don't know Ms. Brennan. But no matter what you two decide, you need to be smart about it."

Thatcher had apparently seen the news about his engagement. He wanted to talk about getting a prenup together or something outlining his and Alena's parenting schedule if they didn't get married. "I said I'd take it under advisement."

"I know what that means coming from you. I've seen richer men—"

"Roger! I'm done with this conversation. If I want your advice or need your services, I'll call you. You've done your due diligence, so rest easy." Andre knew that Roger came from a good place, but sometimes he was overzealous. Which was usually a good thing.

Roger responded but Andre barely heard what he said as Alena stepped into the room.

"I've gotta go," he muttered, hanging up. Wearing a sheer cover-up over a two-piece bathing suit, Alena was like the best present. One he wanted to slowly unwrap, savor.

Her hand went protectively to her bump as she watched, her expression cautious. "I didn't mean to interrupt."

"You can interrupt anytime you want." He'd told her that she had free rein of his house and he hadn't been kidding. It was also why he'd left his office door open; he'd wanted her to know she was welcome. He should have kissed her in that damn parking lot last night, but he'd pulled back, been unsure. Then when they'd gotten back to his place, the moment had passed. And she'd gotten sick. He hadn't thought she'd be feeling remotely into anything. She was the only woman who'd ever made him feel off-balance—even before he found out she'd lied to him. She was so different from his deceased wife, from *any* woman he'd ever known. "Is everything okay?" he asked, standing to round the desk.

"Yes…" She took another hesitant step inside, so unlike the confident woman who'd been in his house before. In this very office.

He tried not to think of what they'd done on this very desk, but failed. His gaze fell to her little bump and he smiled. "It's really visible now."

"Yeah…" She took another step inside, her toenails painted a neon shade of blue. "I just wanted to see if…if maybe we could have Declan and Nika over for dinner? Not that I think I'll be staying here long-term, but just if Brady isn't caught." Her cheeks were red, but he was pretty sure it was from embarrassment this time. He was trying to figure out why she could possibly be embarrassed.

"Of course, anytime you want to have them over." He took a step closer, watched the way her breath hitched—and his gaze fell to her breasts. Pregnancy definitely agreed with her. *Damn.* Her nipples were tight little buds against the thin material of her bathing suit and sheer cover-up. "Do you need anything else?"

Her gaze fell to his mouth for a long moment and she cleared her throat. "Are your security guys inside or outside?"

"Ah, both."

"Oh, okay then…" She took a step back, but he moved, lightning fast, shutting the door.

He didn't want to crowd her, but he wasn't letting her get away from him this time. Not when he'd just now realized why she was here. He turned to face her. "Why are you here, in my office?" he asked, knowing the answer. Or at least guessing. He wanted to hear her say it.

"I…" Her eyes were on his mouth again, all heavy-lidded and hungry. She ever so slightly arched into him, her body language clear enough even if she wasn't vocalizing.

Ah, hell. "If we do this, you know I'm not letting you go." Alena was his. Might as well make that clear. He didn't want secrets or second-guessing between them.

She swallowed hard again. "I think we're probably crazy to even do this, but I don't care. Andre, I want to see where this thing between us can go. For real. And if it doesn't work out, at least we'll know."

"It'll work."

She let out a nervous laugh as he stepped closer. "You sound so sure."

"I make hard decisions every damn day. And the only decision I've ever regretted was when I decided not to go after you four months ago." She hitched in a breath as he leaned down. The scent of her wrapped around him, making him lightheaded. He brushed his lips gently over hers, his entire body jolting at the contact. "We're not doing this on my office floor. Not this time," he murmured against her, his hand cupping her baby bump. When he scooped her up, she let out a little yelp of surprise but curled into him. Warmth spread through him that her instinct was to turn into him, not away from him.

It wouldn't take him long to make it upstairs to his bedroom. To the bed he'd shared with her before.

This time it would be different. There were no lies between them. And never would be again.

CHAPTER TEN

Andre carried Alena up the stairs, moving as fast as he dared with her. With her being pregnant, he was being more careful. Maybe this whole situation was ill advised—even stupid. But he didn't care. He was going with his instinct. His instinct had never let him down before. He'd made millions on his own before he was thirty and now he was pushing forty. Alena was more important than any money, any business deal, and he had to trust that this was the right thing.

Even thinking of walking away from Alena...he knew he would regret it for the rest of his life. He hadn't been lying to her earlier either. Letting her go before—kicking her out of his life—he'd regretted it from the moment he'd done it.

Even in his anger, he'd wanted to go after her. Because while he might not have known all the details, he'd seen the pictures of her parents' bodies. He'd seen what his father had done. He should have gone after her right then and demanded a full explanation. It could have saved them months of being apart.

Out of the corner of his eye, he saw one of his security guys at the top of the stairs, but he ignored the man. He ignored everything but the delicate, complex woman in his arms.

She'd come to his office for sex. Maybe more, but it was impossible to know.

Then she'd gotten nervous. Probably because she thought he would reject her. The very notion was laughable. Which told him she didn't fully understand the power she held over him. That was just as well.

Inside his room, her eyes widened. "It's different."

"Yeah." He'd had his bedroom completely redone in an attempt to remove memories of her. It hadn't worked. The woman was ingrained in his psyche. He remembered exactly how she felt under his fingertips, how she'd arched and moaned into his caresses. How she tasted... And he didn't give a shit about the decor. His erection pushed against his pants but that would have to wait. For now.

Setting her on the edge of the bed, he leaned down, placing his hands on either side of her hips. "Lift your arms," he ordered, not backing up to give her any space.

It was clear his order surprised her, but she did as he said.

Grasping the hem of the sheer cover-up—that did nothing to hide her lean, toned body underneath—he pulled it over her head. The sight of her little bump, completely bared, made his heart skip a beat. He might have had a shitty father, might have done some shady things in his life. But this was one thing he would never regret.

For a moment, it looked as if she wanted to cover herself up, then she clutched onto the edge of the bed, her knuckles going pale.

He frowned. They weren't doing this unless she was completely into it. He pushed up. "We don't have to do anything. There's no rush." It pained him to say it, but he wanted her all in or not at all.

"I know. I definitely plan to take my time." Her voice had dropped a few octaves, the sultry quality sending a jolt to his cock. She still looked unsure. "I want you... I'm just nervous." The last part came out as a whisper.

"I am too." Admitting it was a strain.

He slightly pulled back when she reached for the buckle of his pants—even though it nearly killed him. Because if he was naked or if her mouth was on him... No, he wanted to taste her first. It had been too damn long between them and he wanted to hear those sexy sounds she made while she came.

"Lie back."

She paused for a moment but then scooted back on the bed, her caramel-hued skin glowing against the ivory comforter.

"I've had a lot of dirty fantasies about you," he said, crawling on after her.

Her lips curved up slightly. "Fantasies or memories?"

"Both." They hadn't been together long enough to do remotely everything he'd imagined. And it was a lot. Sliding his hands up her smooth legs, he only stopped when he reached her hips, and pulled her bright blue bathing suit bottom right back down her legs. Her skin looked even darker against the material.

When she unexpectedly cupped herself, slowly teasing her clit, he forgot to breathe for a moment. *Fuck me.*

His erection strained against his pants as he watched her—watching *him* with an almost defiant expression. Daring him to take over. He'd told her he wanted the real her. And it looked as if he was getting her. Hell yeah.

He liked the haughty princess from months ago—and was glad that hadn't changed. He also liked the woman taking control right now.

Grasping one of her legs, he slowly lifted it, keeping his gaze pinned to hers as he pressed his mouth to her inner ankle. She shuddered slightly at the contact, her eyes going even more heavy-lidded.

Before, when they'd been together, the chemistry had been electric. It was no different now as energy sparked between them. And he had a feeling that chemistry was never going to fade.

* * *

For the first time in ages, Alena felt free to be herself. Andre knew the worst things about her and he still wanted her. She'd lied to him. She'd tried to kill his father. There wasn't much worse she could do to push him away. She might hate the path that had thrown the two of them together, but she wasn't sorry she'd met him or was having their child. Not even a little bit.

And she wasn't sorry they were in his bed again. This was something she'd dreamed would happen, but she hadn't even allowed herself to think they'd actually ever end up together again. She'd locked up that hope with the rest of all the bullshit in her life that she compartmentalized in her mind.

As he kissed a path up her inner leg, raking his teeth over her skin, nipping and biting gently—and making the sexiest sounds as he moved higher and higher—all the muscles in her body pulled taut.

She arched her back as he reached her inner thighs, desperate for him to tease his tongue between her slick folds. Instead, it was clear he was enjoying torturing her. She was definitely enjoying it too.

Her inner muscles tightened as he oh so gently pressed his teeth against the most sensitive part of her inner thigh. Not biting exactly, just...teasing. Something she'd learned he was a master at.

But she wanted him to lose control. That was something she'd discovered *she* was a master at—making Andre lose that tight regulator he had on himself when she wanted to feel him thrusting inside her. So often he seemed to be walking a tightrope around her. And she knew he loved being in charge, no matter the situation.

She shifted her hand lower until she started to slide her middle finger inside herself, but lightning fast he grabbed her wrist and completely removed her hand. Taking over again.

Crouched between her spread legs, he pushed up slightly and met her gaze. "No more touching yourself. And take your bikini top off."

Oh God. She *loved* the note of command in his voice. Because even with it, there was still a slight thread of a tremor. Which meant he would most definitely be inside her soon. He was right on that edge himself. Even thinking that had her inner muscles tightening, had more heat blooming between her legs. She was desperate now, desperate to feel him inside her.

She did as he said—ordered—and tossed the scrap of material at him. He let out a light laugh as he batted it away.

Then, without missing a beat, he dipped his head between her legs, and there was no more teasing. No more working her up to it. *Good.* Her nipples beaded into tight buds at the pleasure spiraling through her.

Moaning, she cupped her breasts as his tongue delved between her slick folds. She was so wet for him, so damn needy. No one had ever evoked this reaction in her, had made her want to be vulnerable. But she wanted to give him everything. And not out of guilt. Because she wanted to. Because she...*loved* him. She wasn't even sure when it had happened. At one point she hadn't been sure she was capable of it. Now she knew differently. There would be no one else for her.

When he focused on her clit, teasing his tongue against the sensitive bundle of nerves with a pressure designed to make her crazy, she rolled her hips. On instinct she tried to tighten her legs around his head, but he placed his firm hands against her inner thighs, holding her open for him.

The strength in his grip was evident, but she knew he would never hurt her. Not physically anyway. There was still a small part of her that was scared he was just using her, that he would toss her away after this. But she knew that was her own bullshit. That wasn't in Andre. That wasn't the man she knew.

When he removed one of his hands from her inner thigh, she draped her leg over his back, digging her heel into it even as she clutched the comforter beneath her. Her breasts were so sensitive now she couldn't touch them anymore, just wanted to find release—wanted to feel him inside her. A light sheen of perspiration dotted her skin as her body ached for him.

With each stroke against her folds, pleasure punched out to all her nerve endings. She could easily become addicted to him. All those months ago she'd tried to deny what she felt for him, but it was no use.

When he slid a finger inside her, she automatically tightened around him. She wasn't sure if it was her pregnancy or if it was just being with him, but it wasn't going to take her long to push over the edge.

"Gonna come," she rasped out. "Oh, God."

"My name," he growled against her. "You say only my name."

She'd forgotten what a caveman he was. "Andre."

He focused solely on her clit, teasing and licking and oh God, the pressure. When he added another finger inside her and began stroking, she lost it. Pleasure assaulted her whole body as her climax pushed higher, higher until she plummeted right over that edge into a free fall of pure ecstasy.

He'd learned her body so damn quickly and he clearly hadn't forgotten how easy it was to make her climax.

When he started kissing a path up her body, focusing on her baby bump before moving higher, she spread her legs wider as she reached for him. She wanted to wrap around him, to pull him close.

His fingers, still buried inside her, curled against her inner walls, making her roll her hips as he reached her breasts.

"Clothes off," she murmured, a little drowsy and a lot sated as she struggled with his shirt.

He quickly took over, stripping it and the rest of his clothes off. She hated that his hands weren't on her but took pleasure in watching him move, watching as each piece of clothing was removed to reveal an expanse of hard, muscular perfection. Tall and lean, he was broader than she'd originally expected. He swam, like her, and his arms and pecs showed it. She wanted to touch him everywhere.

His movements were lithe, economical as he shifted back up the bed, covering her. She arched into him, rubbing her breasts against his chest. She was so sensitive it was a pleasure/pain combination. The stimulation made her moan. With his cock right against her entrance she wanted to roll her hips against him, to impale herself on his thick length—but managed to show *some* restraint as he leaned down to kiss her.

As she tasted herself on him, she moaned into his mouth, wrapping her arms and legs around him. She wanted to crawl right out of her skin, to get as close to him as possible.

Need hummed through her, her nerves still buzzing with awareness as he started gently rocking against her folds—but not moving any farther. *Teasing.*

"Inside me now," she mumbled against his mouth.

He pulled back a fraction, his breath warm on her face. The dim light from the nightstand lamp cast shadows over his face, making him look like a sexy, hardened warrior.

"I want to drag this out...but I want inside you more." His voice was savage, more a growl than anything.

Just the sound of his voice turned her on. Another rush of heat pooled between her legs—right as he thrust deep. She tried to move, to shift back against him, but he held her hips firmly in place, the display of his strength only igniting the pilot light of her own desire.

The sensation of being filled by him, of her muscles stretching, set off something inside her. "Move," she demanded. She needed this and knew he did too. She needed him more than her next breath and couldn't believe she'd lived so many months without him.

How had she?

He did that growling thing again before pulling back and out of her. *No—* When he flipped her onto her knees with a carefulness that surprised her, she arched her back as he grabbed her hips, filled her again.

From this position he hit her G-spot perfectly. She clawed at the comforter as he thrust inside her, over and over, his own moans mixed with hers. Then he slowed his pace, in and out, a perfectly steady rhythm—driving her completely crazy.

"I need more." Her voice was as harsh and unsteady as the beat of her heart. He knew exactly what he was doing.

He paused, then began thrusting faster. As he did, he pulled her up, wrapping an arm around her middle, his hand at her throat as he pounded into her. She'd been worried he'd treat her like spun glass but this...this was the Andre she remembered. Demanding, intense, and so very sexual.

Reaching between her legs, she started strumming her clit as he continued thrusting. That was all it took, that little extra stimulation.

When she let go, he let go with her. And she had a feeling he'd been holding back, waiting for her to get her second orgasm. He'd always been like that, so damn determined that she was taken care of first. She should have known then that she had no chance against falling for him. Everything about him was thoughtful when it came to her.

He came inside her in long, hard thrusts. "Alena." Her name came out as a sexy growl.

She lost track of time after they eventually collapsed on the lush comforter. It made a whooshing sound under their tangled, naked bodies. She noticed that he was careful not to land on her, but instead moved to the side, giving her plenty of space. For long moments the only sound in the room was their breathing

"Was I too rough?" Concern laced his words as she finally stretched and rolled on her side to face him.

Smiling, she shook her head as she stretched out next to him. She reached out and ran her fingertips over his muscular chest. "I've missed touching you," she murmured, trailing them all the way down to his half-hard, thick length. The man was insatiable.

He hissed in a breath as he draped an arm over her, pulled her close as he stroked a hand down her spine. "Good. Because I'm not letting you go."

She didn't plan to go anywhere. Scooting closer, she curled into his embrace as she leaned up to meet his lips. She knew they were nowhere near done for now. No, this was only a warm-up. They had a lot of time to make up for.

The thought made her smile against his mouth. She really had no idea how she'd ever thought she could walk away from him. It was as if they'd been given a second chance. And she wasn't going to waste it.

CHAPTER ELEVEN

Cell phone against her ear, Alena sat down at Andre's desk, a smile tugging at her lips. He'd left not too long ago for a business meeting. Last night had solidified everything for her. They were really trying this thing. She was nervous but also excited. It seemed too surreal to even contemplate a real relationship with him, but the thought of not being with him... She wasn't walking away from him.

"You better hurry up, I'm starving," she said to her sister. She'd finally found the energy to get out of bed. All she wanted to do was nap, but Nika had called and Alena actually *was* hungry. For the first time in weeks, she hadn't gotten morning sickness. She hoped she was past that phase. Since she was feeling good, she was going to take the time to catch up on work emails, deal with a few issues with her agent and other admin stuff she'd let slide.

"I'm almost there," Nika said. "What are we having for lunch anyway?"

Alena paused. "I didn't actually think that far ahead. I don't even know what Andre has here. Can you pick up some food?"

Her sister laughed. "You're ridiculous. Are you craving anything?"

"Anything Italian." Something hearty and even a little heavy actually sounded good. She'd been so careful about her food the last couple months, because she hadn't been able to keep anything down. Now she felt as if she could make up for that and eat everything in sight.

"I can definitely do that. So...I can hear the smile in your voice. Did you guys have sex?"

Alena pulled up one of her email accounts and started scanning through the messages as she answered. "Yes. And it was incredible. I think there really is something between us. I felt it before, four months ago. But I didn't want to believe it was real." She still almost didn't want to believe it was real. Everything about him was so damn perfect. She knew that part of the reason she didn't want to accept this was because she'd already lost so much in her life and she was afraid to lose again.

"I'm not going to say I told you so, but I kind of did." Nika laughed lightly. "That man is over the moon for you."

"Yeah, well, the feeling is mutual." Alena hadn't wanted to fall for Andre. She hadn't wanted to *want* him at all. When she saw none of the emails needed an immediate response, she closed the screen and leaned back in the cushioned chair. "So have you decided on a dress yet?"

"Yes, I'm going with the last one that made you cry. But only because the owner of the shop loved it and honestly I'm tired of trying on dresses."

"No," Alena said, straightening in her seat. Her sister wasn't taking any of this seriously. "You have to choose it because it's the perfect one. You're only getting married once." Of that, Alena was certain. Declan was definitely the one for her sister.

"I'm messing with you. I picked it because I love it. I don't care what anyone else thinks."

Alena leaned back in the chair as her stomach growled. "If you don't hurry, I'm going to go clean out Andre's refrigerator."

"Oh my God, you are so impatient. I'm pulling into a shopping center with a few different restaurants and one of them is Italian, so go find something to snack on. I know what you like. Eggplant parm, right?"

"Oooh, yes. And any type of fried appetizer. Something with cheese." She was glad to finally be hungry again, to finally be craving something.

And when Andre got back she planned to jump him. Now that she wasn't getting sick anymore—and now that she'd let herself be open to the idea of Andre—she couldn't wait for a repeat of last night.

Alena saw a little email icon pop up on the bottom of the screen and automatically clicked on it. The second she did, Andre's email account filled the screen, not hers. Of course, because this was his computer. She'd clicked on it without thinking.

Alena started to close out of it but stopped when she saw her name as the subject line for the most recent email. Alena Brennan. There was no mistaking that this email was about her. She shouldn't click on it. But the address was from some attorney. One with a name she vaguely recognized. "Nika, I'm going to do something stupid." She clicked on the message before her sister could respond.

"What are you talking about?" Nika asked.

"Hold on," Alena murmured as she scanned the message, her stomach filling with lead. All guilt at what she was doing dissipated as she read what Andre's attorney had sent him. It was a prenuptial agreement, which she actually understood. He was a wealthy man so it made sense why he would want one if they ever got that far, but there was also a template for a co-parenting agreement, with a whole lot of visitation rights and other garbage that seemed incredibly unfair for her.

It looked as if...he wanted full custody. He'd said he didn't want to involve an attorney. She hadn't even *called* hers because she'd thought they really could figure things out just the two of them. God, she really was stupid. She'd used him, and now, what—he was using her and getting an attorney behind her back? He'd simply wanted to blindside her. Was this how he'd felt when he'd discovered she'd used him? Tears pricked her eyelids, but she blinked them away. Alena cleared her throat. "Can you come get me instead of getting us food? I need to get out of here. Now."

"What's going on?" Nika's voice was sharp now, alert.

"I'll tell you when you get here. And please hurry. I don't want to be here another second."

"Okay. I'll be there in five to ten minutes. But no longer than that. I'm leaving the parking lot right now." Nika didn't press for details, thankfully.

Not that Alena was surprised. That wasn't Nika's way. "Okay, thank you," she said. After they ended the call, Alena left Andre's office and hurried up to his bedroom where he'd moved her clothes only hours before. Nausea swirled inside her and it had nothing to do with morning sickness. How had she had been so dumb? She should have *seen* this coming.

She'd thought he was a decent guy, but he must have decided that... Who knew *what* he'd decided. He was a better liar than she'd ever imagined. More hot tears stung her eyes as she hurried up the stairs. One of the security guys smiled politely at her and she managed to smile back, before swiping away a few stray tears. "Stupid pregnancy hormones," she murmured to him as a way to explain her tears. Not that he'd even asked. But still, she didn't want him to alert Andre that something was wrong. Andre had said he had a meeting and would be back later.

"I understand," he said. "My wife went through the same thing with both of ours."

Smiling politely while her heart broke, she continued on to Andre's room and quickly packed her bag. She didn't have much here, thankfully. And if she had, she would have just left it. Once she had everything together, she'd just started to call her sister when she received a text.

At the security gate. Want me to drive up or wait outside the estate?

Alena texted her sister back quickly. *Meet me by the front door, I'll be out in one minute.*

The walk down the driveway would have been long and she could admit that she just wanted to get in her sister's car and leave. Then cry. And probably sleep.

True to her word, Nika pulled up as Alena stepped out onto the front steps. By the time she'd descended to the bottom, Nika was out and had the trunk open. Alena's bag wasn't even big but she tossed it in and got into the passenger seat.

"So...what the heck is going on?" Nika asked as she steered down the driveway.

"I'm a dumbass," Alena muttered.

"Seriously, you went from happy to upset in the span of a short phone call. What happened?" Nika asked as she reached the end of the long driveway.

The gate was wide open and Alena was glad to be able to leave without having to talk to Andre. Because right now she didn't trust herself to not have another stupid hormonal breakdown. She didn't want to appear weak in front of him. "I was using Andre's computer and when an email notice popped up I automatically clicked on it. I was going to close the program down when I saw my name as the subject line. It's—"

As Nika steered out onto the quiet street, a giant van rammed into the back of them. Alena jolted forward under the impact as her sister let out a cry of surprise. All her muscles went tight as the car flew forward. Nika turned the wheel, trying to gain control as the van slammed into them again, sending them into a tailspin.

This was no accident!

As the back of Nika's car hit a telephone pole, the seat belt jerked tight across Alena again. She let out a cry of pain and grasped onto the center console and door to steady herself. The belt wasn't directly across her belly but she still had to shove back panic. What if—

The van stopped ten feet in front of them and when the driver's side door opened, she blinked.

It was Harold Brady. Declan had called and told her and Andre that the New Orleans PD had gotten a tip that he'd been seen in New Orleans. Near her house there. Which made sense that he'd go to her known residence. The police there were staking it out. He couldn't be in Miami. She looked over at her sister, who was shaking her head, but seemed otherwise fine.

"Are you okay?" Alena asked as raw fear slammed through her. "Because we need to get the hell out of here now."

"Yeah…" She tried to start the car but the ignition made a clicking sound.

A waterfall of panic started to punch through Alena as Brady stalked toward them. Wearing simple jeans and a T-shirt, he could be anyone on the street. But she knew how dangerous he was. At his side, he held a weapon. A gun.

"Oh, God. Nika..." Scrambling, she reached for her fallen purse. There was only pepper spray in there but if she could get close enough to him she was going to use it. She fumbled once as she tried to pull it out.

Nika pulled a gun out of the center console as Alena's fingers clasped around her pepper spray.

Of course Nika would have a gun for protection. Alena wasn't thinking clearly. She couldn't believe Brady was heading toward them. It was something right out of a nightmare.

"You're mine, Alena!" the man screamed as he stalked even closer.

Alena felt almost frozen in place as he reached the hood of the car. "Nika—"

"Crouch down as low as you can—"

He jumped on the hood, weapon raised right at her.

Pop. Pop. Pop.

Brady froze for a moment, almost as if his body was suspended in air, when suddenly the string holding him snapped. He slammed forward, his entire body hitting the windshield and hood. His eyes were wide but unseeing as blood trickled down on the glass, a small stream at first.

"Did you..." No, of course Nika hadn't shot him. It would have killed their eardrums. That was when she saw the swarm of Andre's security guys moving in on the car like the trained experts they were.

One of them was at her door, knocking insistently on the window. Feeling numb, she fumbled with the door lock even as Nika opened her own.

The man said something to her, asked her if she was all right. She must have nodded that she was, but all she could think about was getting to her sister. Ignoring the man, she hurried to where Nika was on the other side of the vehicle and pulled her into her arms.

"I'm sorry," she sobbed out, shaking all over. She couldn't look at Brady's body.

"Oh, honey, you have nothing to be sorry for." Nika rubbed her back in soft little circles.

"Not for this," she rasped out. She was sorry for everything, for the way she'd dragged Nika into her need for revenge. Nika might have forgiven her, or even be okay with it. But too many emotions swelled inside Alena right now, and seeing a dead guy on her sister's car hood, knowing that this man might have ambushed them somewhere else and taken Nika from her... That she could have lost her baby! The tears kept coming. "Oh, God. I'm so fucking sorry." She couldn't stop crying as sobs racked her body. She needed to find out if her baby was okay but she couldn't let go of her sister.

For years she'd been compartmentalizing her life, and everything was fracturing and blistering up to the surface. And right up until this moment, she wasn't completely certain how she felt about her pregnancy.

Icing on this shitty cake: Andre had lied to her. And that cut deep too.

The only thing she knew without a shadow of a doubt was that she wanted to be a mother. She was still terrified that she'd screw it up, but she wanted the chance.

The sound of sirens rang out in the distance and soon she and Nika found themselves being checked out by EMTs and then driven to the police station. There would be questions to answer but they were alive. And a madman was dead.

She finally stopped crying halfway to the police station. And she couldn't dredge up any emotions for Brady. All she cared was that her wonderfully brave sister was alive. And they'd walked away from this unhurt, that she and the baby were okay. It all seemed so surreal, had happened so fast.

Just another reminder that life changed in a second. Something she didn't need to be reminded of. Her life had changed drastically at the age of ten. And that change had shaped the woman she had become. She might not want to do this on her own, but she would be a strong single mom. Andre wasn't going to take anything away from her.

* * *

Andre barely kept his panic in check as he followed the uniformed officer down a long hallway. He passed men and women in uniform, and some in suits, but he tuned them all out. His only focus was on getting to Alena. He knew she was alive, unharmed.

But he needed to see it for himself, needed to hold her in his arms.

"This is it," the woman murmured as she knocked once on the door. She opened it and stepped back for Andre to enter.

His gaze was immediately drawn to Alena, who sat in front of a desk next to her sister, in a surprisingly lush office. Her eyes were red, puffy, and she looked away from him.

Nika and Declan occasionally worked with the police, though he had no idea how they assisted the cops. And at this moment he didn't care. But he assumed it was why they'd been put in such a nice office to wait.

Declan, who was on his cell phone, nodded once at him before ending his call and shoving his phone in his pocket.

Andre shut the door behind him and made a move toward Alena. To his surprise, she remained sitting where she was, and just looked at him with the most neutral expression. Cold, almost. If it wasn't for her red eyes he'd wonder if anything had happened to her at all.

Maybe she was in shock? "I got here as soon as I could," he said, kneeling in front of her. He took her hands in his, but she stiffened. "I know what I was told, but are you okay? Is our baby okay?"

"I'm okay. So is our baby." Placing a protective hand on her bump, she flicked a quick glance at her sister, who then murmured that they were going to give the two of them privacy.

When Declan and Nika shut the door behind them, Alena pulled her hands away from him. "You didn't need to come down here."

"Are you fucking kidding me? Why wouldn't I come down here? What the hell is going on?" One of his security guys had told him that she'd packed a bag and had tossed it into her sister's trunk before leaving. Before all hell had broken loose. Andre had thought maybe the guy had been confused.

"I just meant that I'm okay. And I'm going to be staying at my sister's house tonight. I just need some space. So much has happened today."

He sat in the chair opposite her, stunned by her words. After last night, he'd thought they had cemented a real bond. They'd even talked about it, about her staying at his place indefinitely, about figuring things out between them. "Stay with me."

The smile she gave him was completely fake and didn't reach her eyes. "Not tonight." The way she said it, it sounded like *not ever* in his head. "I've been looked over by the EMTs and I have an appointment set up with Dr. Freeman this week."

"You're more than welcome to stay with me." In fact, he would prefer it. He never wanted her to leave. Something he thought she would know by now. Especially after what they'd shared.

She gave him another one of those fake smiles. "Of course, I know." Standing, she wrapped her arms around herself, clearly keeping a wall up between them. "Nika and I are actually done here. We were about to head out when you called Declan."

Why was she acting this way? She was completely different from the woman he'd held in his arms last night. The one who'd come apart in his arms. "I called you first."

"I don't have my phone on me. I think it's still in Nika's car."

"I can drive you to your sister's." Because he wanted to continue this conversation, to figure out what the hell was going on. She was pissed at him. He hadn't realized it at first but now he did. She was angry about something. Considering everything she'd just been through, he didn't want to push too hard. But there was a thinly veiled anger under the fake smile. As if she wanted to punch him right in the throat.

She let out a light laugh. Definitely fake. And it grated against his nerves. "That's not necessary. It wouldn't make any sense when I can just ride with Nika."

"When are you coming back?" he asked bluntly.

She lifted a shoulder and glanced away from him, clearly avoiding answering the question. "We'll talk about it later."

Before he could push, the door opened. Declan nodded once at him. "Nika is ready to get home. Alena, have you decided what you're doing?"

She brushed past Andre, not bothering to give him a second glance. "I'm ready too."

"Did something else happen with Alena?" Andre asked Declan quietly as he followed him out into the hallway. The women were up ahead of them, out of earshot.

"I don't know. She's been very quiet since I arrived at the station. She just said she wanted to go home with us."

Fuck. Fuck this whole situation. There was no way he could push her now even if he didn't want to let her go. "Take care of her. And if you need anything from me, let me know."

Declan nodded and shook his hand once. "My cell is glued to me. Call me if you can't get hold of her."

In other words, if Alena decided to ignore his calls, he could call Declan. At least that was what he took that to mean. "Okay. Thank you."

Watching her leave was one of the hardest things he'd ever done. He wanted to go after her and demand answers. But she'd just seen someone killed. He wouldn't have thought it would have bothered her so much, considering some of the things she'd done. But people dealt with things in different ways. Maybe... Hell, he couldn't even analyze what was going on in her head right now.

He just knew that he didn't like the way she'd been pulling away from him, the way she'd decided not to come home with him. With this threat gone, he'd assumed... He scrubbed a hand over the back of his neck.

When he took in his surroundings and realized he was still standing in the lobby of the police station, he got it together. He needed to get out of here. And figure out what to do about Alena. He'd told her that he wasn't letting her go, and he'd been serious.

He wanted her at his side and in his life forever.

CHAPTER TWELVE

Alena couldn't stop the nerves humming through her as she sat in Dr. Freeman's waiting room. There were only two other women, both pregnant, and Nika, who was filling out Alena's paperwork for her. She'd been a mess the past two days, and was grateful for her sister's presence now.

She'd wanted to ask Andre to come with her, but they hadn't talked in a couple days and she was still feeling conflicted about what she'd seen. She *should* talk to him about that email, but she didn't want to hear him lie to her. She didn't want to deal with anything right now. She wanted to stick her head in the sand like an ostrich and just ignore the outside world. Super mature, she thought wryly.

Ignoring everything was pretty difficult to do since Harold Brady had been killed right in front of her—and he'd been trying to murder her. He'd apparently called in the tip about himself being near her New Orleans home. He'd wanted her guard down. The police had found a disturbing manifesto-type letter in the hovel he'd been staying in, in Miami. He hadn't been planning to let her live. No, she'd apparently "betrayed" him by becoming engaged to someone else instead of waiting for him. Because in his deranged mind she'd been waiting for him to get out of prison—even though he never would have gotten out on parole. As far as the Miami PD could tell, him showing up at the time she was leaving with her sister was luck. Or he could have been staking out the house. They weren't sure and would likely never know.

The media was having a field day, dissecting him and his intentions, but somehow Declan had made sure no one knew where she was staying. And he'd driven both her and Nika to this appointment and was outside keeping an eye on the parking lot in case any nosy reporter showed up hoping to get a picture of her leaving.

When Nika poked her in the arm with the top of her pen, Alena blinked. "What?"

"Have you heard a word I've said?"

"No."

Nika pointed to the part on the paper where it asked if she was single, married, engaged, etc. "I made an executive decision and said that you're engaged."

Alena glanced down at the ring on her left-hand finger. She felt like a fraud wearing it, but had decided that if she was seen in public, it was better that she had the ring on. Less crap for her to deal with that way if the media assumed she was still engaged. Her agent had made a generic statement about how she was spending time with her family and just wanted privacy.

"Are you ever going to finish that conversation we started in my car?" Nika asked pointedly as a nurse stepped inside and called for one of the other women.

Alena knew exactly which conversation her sister referred to. "Yes. But not today."

Nika just gave her a frustrated look but Alena didn't have the energy to get into anything. Especially not here with someone sitting in the room with them. Her sister handed her the clipboard and papers. "I've filled everything out," she said, standing. "And you can get mad at me later but..." She nodded at the entryway and Alena turned to see Andre, of all people, walking inside, his expression wary.

He nodded once at Nika—who left, *the traitor*—before sitting down next to Alena. "How are you feeling?" he asked quietly.

Her spine went rigid. "No nausea today." She didn't know what else to say. And she nearly jumped when the nurse opened the door and called her name. As she stood, Andre stood with her.

Even if she was hurt by his actions, she wasn't going to keep him out of the room. She wanted him involved in their child's life, even if he wasn't involved in hers. Smiling at the nurse, even though it strained her to do so, she handed the clipboard over as she stepped into the private hallway.

Taking her by surprise, Andre took her hand in his, linking their fingers together. She didn't stop him, but only because she didn't want to draw any attention to herself.

"You'll be in room five today," the nurse said, as they stopped at a room marked *five*. "Dr. Freeman will be with you in just a bit." The woman's smile was warm as she led them inside.

With an exam table, an ultrasound machine and black-and-white framed art against pale grayish-blue walls, the room was very soothing.

"They're doing an ultrasound today?" Andre asked, looking around the room curiously.

"Yes. I'm at the point where we can find out the sex of the baby." Her voice was almost monotone. She couldn't dredge up the energy for anger right now. She was absolutely drained emotionally—and hurt. God, she was *hurt*. She hadn't wanted to eat at all the last couple days and had only done so because she needed to.

His eyes widened. "Do you want to find out?"

"Kind of. Yes." Though she didn't care what she had, just that the baby was healthy.

He shoved his hands in his pockets, looking lost. "I can't believe we're having a baby."

She sat on the edge of the exam table. "I know." Even with the pain of his betrayal, she was still excited.

"Why haven't you returned my calls the last couple days?" he asked softly.

"Because…" She swallowed hard, trying to find the right words. She hadn't even been able to tell her sister why. She'd holed up in the guest room and slept, ate and read books, avoiding social media altogether. And she'd most definitely ignored phone calls from Andre.

The door opened then, and Dr. Freeman stepped inside. Her long black hair was pulled back into a braid and she had very little makeup on, but she was still the same stunning woman from the gala. She smiled warmly at the two of them. "How are the parents-to-be today?"

Even thinking of herself as a parent made Alena feel weird. It was still too surreal. They both murmured "Good" at the same time.

"Great," the doctor said. Then she asked Alena to scoot back on the exam table and lift up her shirt. She went over everything she was going to do, then asked, "Do you guys want to know the sex of the baby?"

Alena looked at Andre. She could see in his eyes that he wanted to know. "What do you think?" she asked him.

"It's up to you."

"No, it's up to us. I would like to." *And I want to know what that email was about.*

He let out a little breath of relief and nodded, a small smile pulling at his lips. "Me too."

"All right, let's do this," Dr. Freeman said, dimming the lights in the room.

Andre stood by Alena's head, and took one of her hands in his as Dr. Freeman spread a clear gel on her exposed stomach. It was cold, but not uncomfortable. And as she pressed the wand to Alena's bump, they all looked at the screen.

Alena sucked in a breath at the site of the little peanut, which looked more like a baby than the blob she'd seen at her last ultrasound. Andre squeezed her hand gently but she didn't turn to look at him because she couldn't tear her gaze from the screen.

"Give me just a second," Dr. Freeman murmured more to herself than them. Then she let out a little *aha* sound. "It's definitely a girl," she said, smiling at the two of them.

Alena's throat tightened as she stared at the screen. A girl. Holy crap, this was so real. Tears welled in her eyes, and this time it had nothing to do with hormones. She was just happy.

"I'm going to get a few pictures for you guys and then I'll give you some privacy."

Andre wiped away Alena's tears as the door shut behind Dr. Freeman. "Whatever I've done to upset you, I'm sorry. How can I make it right?" There was a desperation in his voice that nearly undid her.

Either he really was the best liar or... She couldn't even think of a good reason for that email. She didn't want to have this conversation now, but there was no way around it. "I wasn't trying to snoop or anything, but when I was on your computer a new email icon popped up. I automatically clicked on it because it's the same icon as on my computer. I started to close it out, but stopped when I saw my name. And then I definitely snooped and I read a letter from your attorney—"

Andre swore softly then yanked his phone out of his pocket. Wordlessly, he typed in his code then pulled up something before turning the screen toward her. It took only a second to realize it was his response to the email. And the response had been sent before she'd read the original one. The message hadn't been unread, so she knew Andre had seen it that day. She just hadn't realized he'd already responded.

I've told you more than once, this isn't necessary. Like I said before, you've done your due diligence where I'm concerned. Now drop it or I'm going to find a new attorney. We've been friends for a long time, but I'm sick of this shit. I don't want a prenup and I don't want you to bring up anything about Alena Brennan again unless I bring it up first.

She stared at it, reading it one more time before handing the phone back to him. Elation intermixed with regret swirled inside her. "I thought..."

He pocketed his phone and took her hand in his again. "It makes more sense now why you've been so distant."

"I'm sorry. I saw that message, and the prenup doesn't bother me. I'll sign whatever you want—"

"Wait, you'll sign a prenup? Does that mean—"

"No, I just meant—"

"I'm pretty sure I know exactly what you meant. You just said you'll marry me." He crushed his mouth to hers, stealing her breath in the best way possible. When he pulled back they were both breathing hard as he gently cupped her cheeks. "And I don't want a prenup."

Alena didn't want to think or talk about that. Not when the man she loved hadn't betrayed her. If anything, he was more perfect than before, something she hadn't thought possible. "God, I'm so sorry. I should have trusted you, should have talked to you."

"From this point forward, no more running away. If I've done something, or if you think I've done something, talk to me. And I'll talk to you." His voice cracked on the last word.

Making more tears well in her eyes. "I will, I promise. And no running. I really am sorry," she whispered.

"It's done. I was angry but...I understand why you'd be upset. Let's start fresh."

She nodded, swiping away her tears. "I want our engagement to be real," she whispered. "I love you, Andre. I fell so hard and so fast for you that I thought it couldn't be real. The last two days... I've been heartbroken. I thought..." It didn't matter what she thought now. Because she'd been wrong. "I don't want to waste any more time second-guessing myself or us."

"I love you too." He cupped her cheeks again with his big hands, his expression so warm she wanted to melt.

"I feel like we're crazy for even being together."

"I don't care. Because I'm crazy for you."

"That's so cheesy," she whispered even as more tears welled up. He got that panicked look again and she laughed. "These are happy tears, I swear."

He pressed his forehead to hers. "I can't believe we're having a girl. I'm going to have to lock her up until she's thirty."

"Pretty sure that's not happening," she said, laughing.

"Will you come home with me today? And we don't have to stay at the estate. I can sell it and we can buy something together."

"I love your place."

"Then it's ours."

"Andre—"

"No. If you move in there, it becomes ours."

Oh hell, she had to force the tears back. "Well I love it. But I don't care where we live." The truth was, she would prefer Miami since it was close to her sister, but she had to take his feelings into account as well. "If you want to live in Vegas or even Biloxi, we can."

"I've been shifting a lot of things around the past few months. I can work in Miami just as easily as Vegas or Biloxi. I'll still have to travel, but I'll be in Miami the majority of the week. And…I didn't plan to bring it up today, but I wanted to talk to you about a potential business relationship."

"You mean between us?"

"Yes. I'm looking for a new spokesperson/face for my casinos. And I think you're perfect for it. It's a ten-year contract."

Her eyes widened. She'd have to run things by her agent and there would be a lot to figure out, but… "That's incredible."

"One of the stipulations is that you sleep in my bed every night." His voice was low and husky.

She giggled at that even as heat pooled between her legs. "I think we need to get out of here. Two days without you and I've been going crazy."

"Same here. I don't want to wait to get married, Alena." His voice was suddenly serious.

"Okay...but we have to wait until after Nika's wedding."

"As long as it's before this little girl is born," he said, cupping her stomach.

"I didn't realize you were so traditional."

"Neither did I." The heat and hunger were back in his gaze.

She was ready to get out of here and back to his place. Immediately. She might have made a lot of mistakes where he was concerned but she wasn't going to screw this up. Her need for revenge had almost ruined her life. She wouldn't let her baggage get in the way of what she and Andre—and their daughter—could have. And she was going to have to stop being so damn suspicious and just accept the love he was offering. That in itself felt like a feat, but she could accept that this was real, that they were meant to be together.

EPILOGUE

One year later

Alena sat down next to Nika on the bench swing by the pool, smiling at the sight of her sister holding Alena's baby girl. Grace was so tiny and the perfect mix of her and Andre. "I swear you have the magic touch with her," she murmured.

"I love her so much." Nika gently kissed her head before continuing to rock her. "I can't believe how much she sleeps."

Alena snorted. "She's fooling you. I swear she puts on a show for her aunt. Which is fine with me because the only time she sleeps solidly is around you."

"Are you ready to let her have a sleepover at my house?" Nika asked slyly.

Grace was a little over seven months old now and Alena thought she might be ready to spend a night away from her. Maybe. "I don't know," she said, laughing. She completely trusted her sister, but being away from Grace felt weird. "I'm pretty sure Andre isn't."

As if he knew he was being talked about, the sliding glass door opened behind them and he and Declan stepped outside. Andre's sister and Declan's brothers would be there soon. As well as Nika's father-in-law.

They were having a Sunday night dinner, and this weekend Andre had volunteered their place since Kiley was in town.

"Andre isn't what?" he asked, before kissing Alena on the top of her head and sitting in the lounge chair right next to them.

"Nika wants to keep Grace for the night."

"We've already got a crib and everything," Declan said as he sat on the other side of Nika, a beer in hand.

"Crib?" Alena asked.

Nika rolled her eyes. "We were going to tell you tonight, but apparently that's my husband's way of letting you know that I'm pregnant."

"Oh my gosh, congratulations!" She wrapped a gentle arm around her sister's shoulder, not wanting to jostle her too much.

Nika smiled and looked down at her niece. "I'm getting plenty of practice with this little one."

"That's fantastic, you guys. You're going to make great parents." Andre smiled at the two of them, a much more relaxed version of the man he was during the work week. He was so busy, but he made time for Alena and Grace. Always.

She'd ended up signing that contract for the casino spokesperson gig, but wouldn't start for another five months. She was privileged enough to have been able to take a long maternity leave and she had no regrets. But she knew that definitely wasn't the case for everyone, which was why she'd been working with Andre's assistant to set up better childcare programs at all of his casinos. His employees kept odd hours and now they were trying to make sure that any parents who worked for him would have an easier time by having on-site care. He already had paid maternity leave in place, but he was taking it one step further.

"I think we'd be okay with letting Grace stay the night," he said, surprising Alena.

The truth was, while it would probably be hard, she knew her child would be safe with Nika and Declan. She had no doubts about that. And she could definitely use a free night with her husband. She loved saying that word, *husband.*

They'd gotten married about a month after Nika had. Andre had been so insistent on them being married before she gave birth, not that she'd resisted. Of all the people in the world, she sometimes still couldn't believe she'd fallen for the son of her enemy, but she was incredibly grateful that she had.

Because he was perfect for her and an incredible father, if crazy overprotective. Which was something she could understand.

"All right, if we're going to let you take Grace tonight, I'm getting a little cuddle time." She held out her arms, making her sister smile. From the time Alena was ten, she'd been both mother and sister to Nika. Yes, their uncle had raised them, but she had been the one who looked out for her little sister. Now they were both all grown up and she knew her sister was going to make an incredible mother. She wondered if their child would have Nika and Declan's psychic gifts or a combination of both. Not that it mattered, as long as the baby was healthy.

Nika handed Grace over and stood, stretching. "I'm going to go grab a glass of wine. Did you want anything?"

"A bottle of water would be nice, thanks."

As Nika and Declan headed inside, Andre moved, sitting next to her. He wrapped his arm around her shoulders and ran a gentle hand over Grace's cheek. "I'm going to miss Grace, but I'm ready for some—"

"Sleep?"

He barked out a laugh. "I was going to say sex, but sex *and* sleeping in sounds like heaven."

She leaned over and brushed her lips over his. Automatically heat pooled between her legs. This man had the ability to take her from zero to sixty in a second. The last few months had definitely been difficult with lack of sleep, but it had brought them closer together. He'd mentioned getting a nanny, but she wasn't to that point yet. She wasn't sure if she ever would be. It took a lot of trust to let someone she didn't know into her house and around her child. And she wasn't afraid to admit that she still had trust issues in general where people were concerned. She figured that would never go away, not with her background. And she knew she couldn't protect Grace forever, but for right now, she was going to do her best.

"We haven't had hot tub sex in a while," she murmured.

He laughed and brushed his lips over hers again. "Or shower sex."

"It's on tonight," she whispered as she heard the sliding glass door open behind them.

Andre wrapped his arm just a little tighter around her as the others joined them.

She leaned into him, savoring his comforting hold. She'd certainly never expected a man like Andre in her life. She'd never expected to be where she was right now. In truth, she'd worried that her quest for revenge might kill her. Now she was glad that she'd survived, that she had a whole life ahead of her, with wonderful people she loved more than anything.

She laid her head on her husband's shoulder and looked down at the perfection of her baby girl. Life was good. And she was going to hold on to this life forever.

—The End—

Thank you for reading Tempting Danger. If you don't want to miss any future releases, please feel free to join my monthly newsletter. Find the signup link on my website: http://www.katiereus.com

ACKNOWLEDGMENTS

Thank you to all my wonderful readers who read Retribution and insisted that Alena and Andre get a story too! It took a couple years, but it's finally here. For my fantastic editor, Julia, thank you for your attention to detail. For Sarah, thank you for all the behind-the-scenes work you do. Kari, you're the best and I'm so grateful that you read the early versions of all my books! Chudney, thank you for answering my questions! Jaycee, thank you for another beautiful cover. You've outdone yourself this time. And as always, I'm incredibly grateful to my family and to God.

COMPLETE BOOKLIST

Red Stone Security Series
No One to Trust
Danger Next Door
Fatal Deception
Miami, Mistletoe & Murder
His to Protect
Breaking Her Rules
Protecting His Witness
Sinful Seduction
Under His Protection
Deadly Fallout
Sworn to Protect
Secret Obsession
Love Thy Enemy
Dangerous Protector
Lethal Game

Deadly Ops Series
Targeted
Bound to Danger
Chasing Danger (novella)
Shattered Duty
Edge of Danger
A Covert Affair

Redemption Harbor Series
Resurrection
Savage Rising
Dangerous Witness

Moon Shifter Series
Alpha Instinct
Lover's Instinct
Primal Possession
Mating Instinct
His Untamed Desire
Avenger's Heat
Hunter Reborn
Protective Instinct
Dark Protector
A Mate for Christmas

Darkness Series
Darkness Awakened
Taste of Darkness
Beyond the Darkness
Hunted by Darkness
Into the Darkness
Saved by Darkness

ABOUT THE AUTHOR

Katie Reus is the *New York Times* and *USA Today* bestselling author of the Red Stone Security series, the Moon Shifter series and the Deadly Ops series. She fell in love with romance at a young age thanks to books she pilfered from her mom's stash. Years later she loves reading romance almost as much as she loves writing it.

However, she didn't always know she wanted to be a writer. After changing majors many times, she finally graduated summa cum laude with a degree in psychology. Not long after that she discovered a new love. Writing. She now spends her days writing dark paranormal romance and sexy romantic suspense.

For more information on Katie please visit her website: www.katiereus.com. Also find her on twitter @katiereus or visit her on facebook at: www.facebook.com/katiereusauthor.

Made in the USA
Columbia, SC
07 May 2018